First Edition

ISBN 1-903110-23-8

Cover Illustration by Owen Benwell

Cover Design by Owen Benwell

Published in 2005 by
Wrecking Ball Press
24 CAVENDISH SQUARE • HULL • ENGLAND . HU3 1SS

Daithidh MacEochaidh

Travels with Chinaski

**for ma father, Michael Keogh,
who wonders why I bother with poetry**

Apologia:

(Ripped, mangled and disagreed with from Aristophanes -- The Frogs:)
We have a duty to teach what is right and proper.
Schoolchildren have teachers.
Grown ups have the poets.
Give me a bowl of pea soup -- any day.

Other Titles by Daithidh MacEochaidh:

Like a Dog to its Vomit
Half a Pint of Tristram Shandy
Solipsism for Beginners
Ramraid
Liquorish Durg (how northern naturalism lost its false teeth)
Shakespeare Ate My Sonnet
Islands in Time

Beginnings as a Means to an End

You don't forget the first time you meet Henry Chinaski.
I was struggling to get up, to wipe the sick from my
bedspread, to grab just what was left of the insides of my
head. He was there, waiting patiently for me, a beer in his
hand, some nubbins of a cigarette, hung from his bottom
lip; a lip bruised like a plum and not for picking.

I don't forget the first time I met Henry Chinaski,
stronger than ma first taste of champagne, sour mash
bourbon or kiss of cunt. Those sent me; they filled ma
mouth right up, stung ma head with some smell of life
that I wanted to savour till death. That first girl I kissed,
pushing aside her pants with ma tongue, licking ma way
in like some serpent, Adam and Eve bound and not caring
a fig for Jehovah -- the world's first absentee landlord.
Some taste of honey, rolling round ma tongue, some bud of
clit, banged up against the tip of ma tongue; some sweet
seam of stink -- delved deep as I could. Loved that first
taste of woman, wiped ma whole face with it.

But that sharp stink of Chinaski almost took it all away,
when I found him seated in ma chair like some rotten fox,
dead with cunning, dead with advice. He was there in ma
room and he said it was time to take a walk into what we
had in our neighbourhood for sunlight.

'S about eight hours out there the sun's giving you this
day, don't waste it, don't forget it, don't try to hide from it -
- believe you me, you'll regret it when you dead, said
Chinaski. He meant every word. He was mean with every
word, like he had them stored up for this dull-brown day
in mid-fall, mauled by the sound of children playing
cowboys, playing Star Wars, playing up, playing down the
street and hollering with the raw instinct of the immortal
present. There was everything in Chinaski's words, but

still I shook the dried lumps of sick off my bed, settled
back down into the pit of it all, not knowing what to feel,
wanting to spit Chinaski's words out of ma mouth,
wanting to give ma semi a pull, yet wondering if Chinaski
would mind. He seemed something of a puritan all told.

Go ahead, said Chinaski, I'm out of here for a paper
anyways. There's a hot race meeting today and you could
do worse than back a winner for me.

I didn't hear the door go. Mindst, I never heard this bum
walk in and sit down on ma only seat, just woke up and
there he was like a part-time succubus hovering over ma
bed, boasting the sickly sweet hum of the newly dead.
Even when he'd gone, fag-ash falling from his fingers,
I could still taste him, I could hockle him to the far wall,
to the cracked mirror above ma chest of drawers; I could
do all these things and still taste. There was something
about him in the breath I took, as a little asthmatically,
I made it to squirt some pumped up cum over ma sheets,
over the spiral of stomach and chest hairs. It was not
question of smell, but ever a question of taste when it
came to Chinaski.

Singing some old blues, I rubbed it in. Seemed to rub
Chinaski in too, but thought a hot shower and a few days
free from drink could cure it, wash it right out and let me
sample those eight hours or so of sullen autumn. When
you're nursing hangovers, it gets crazy what you can
think. It gets so that it makes great sense. It gives you an
expanding perspective on all the hurting madness you
ever felt and thought before. Mad, drunk, spunk, cunt,
sunk...I laughed at with the words tumbling, leap-frogging
and cartwheeling through ma head, even as I wondered if
I'd left that half bottle of champagne in the fridge.

Always wonder that and e'er am I disappointed. I
wondered if Chinaski even knew the way to the paper
shop and what he thought of Asian sole-traders.

10

I wondered if I could fit another wank into the morning, afore that wide-head would beckon me to the sink, the shower and the cleaners on Fifth Ave where all of we poor people gan. I tried, had mad hot exotic thoughts, deep dirty monkey fucking, the sad twisted eye of ma prick weeping, weeping for something more than solitary pleasures.

Yet, from that day, I wasn't alone. I had Chinaski. I spat him, shat him, I smeared him across the page: he was there for me.

Fire Walking

So he was back, through the partition, in the kitchen
setting fire to bread, smoking me out, fumes of stale fat
burning from the grill, setting ma eyes to smart. I would
have slept it out, but Mrs Woodhall from down the
corridor came and rapped at ma door. She said, Hey, don't
you know something is burning in there? I said that I did
know, that a friend of mine was making toast, but not very
well, but that did she know that her husband was poking
a fifteen year old. She slammed the door in ma face, which
I thought was something unusual since it was ma door. I
hollered after the swiftly retreating form, to leave ma door
alone, that if she so much as looked at ma door again, I'd
kill one of her pissy cats -- kill two cats, skin 'em and wear
them for handcrafted slippers with tails at the back. All
this I hollered to this small form of shrinking woman,
through a shut door; her door, slammed in ma face with
more of a respect for the traditions and conventions of the
sit-com or romantic comedy, but I felt no better. Felt no
worse either mindst, guess I just didn't have ma feeling
head on that day.

Chinaski came to that more traditional slammed door,
said, Get your sorry ass back in here. Putting an arm
around ma shoulder, he dragged me back to that strip of
sink, hob and grill that was ma kitchen. Chinaski said,
Son, I think that your toast is done.

Christ, did Chinaski ever under-exaggerate. Ma toast was
in a worse state than when I said goodbye to ma
grandfather at the crematorium. Laughed at that, because
he'd been quite a smoker and I allus laugh at ma own
jokes, stops me bumming for cheap laughs elsewhere. That
toast tasted like ashtrays, but I couldn't afford to waste it
being all the bread I owned and today I had to eat
something. Sullen consolation: I didn't have to like it.

Chinaski shrugged philosophically, as I shared ma repast with him, as he stuck the kettle on to boil, to try again to raise some tea taint from the leaves still stuck in ma white-cracked teapot, held together by consolidated tannins and rich, hot-caffeine resistant bacteria.

Chinaski made breakfast and if he wasn't quite Jeeves, he was still a handy man to have around, even as I couldn't help resenting him being there, trying on some of ma clothes, shitting in ma bog, using ma soap in the shower, leaving his greying pubes all choked up in it and not for shifting. Hated him for that, but I never asked him to go, just refused to use that bar of soap any longer.

I laughed. Chinaski brewed up, sloshed off something warm into the cups, we had it black, `cos I like it that way and I had no milk that wasn't seriously off. Still I laughed. His rolly had gone out and he stuck his head down to light the doff off the gas and burnt his left eyebrow as the cooker had one of those rare spats, some sudden spurt of flame. Chinaski batting himsel' in the eye, cursing like a Tourettic nun in a confessional, swearing blind that he'd lick me for that. I don't ken what he reckoned the `that' was, but it made ma face crack with smiles. And, really, he wasn't so sore, just smoked his tab, complained about the lack of sugar in his tea, as he settled back to read all about the runners in that race he was so hoped up on. I laughed all the way to ma next bite of toast. It sure was burnt.

We would have sat there a lot longer, but there was an argument next door, just along the corridor, by that slammed door I was talking about. Mr and Mrs Woodhall were ripping lumps out of each other. I just hoped that it was true what they said about him and the free-paper girl. He seemed to be paying dear if it was just a rumour. Chinaski cracked a smile, threw his thumb over his shoulder in the direction of the shower, knew it was time that we moved on. There was a little less sunshine in the

day, the race was nearing and I seemed to be out of
shampoo. Not a good time to run out of pharmaceuticals:
hair and clothes matted with last night's sick. I dithered
in ma dirt, laughing nay longer.

Chinaski said, Here let me show you how.

He did just that. He made me stand in the lukewarm
shower, fully clothed, as he squirted washing up liquid
into ma hair. I shampooed with that and it wasn't over.
He threw in cupfuls of washing powder and I rubbed it
well in and really washed up in there. I came out clean,
smelling of dangerous, environmentally unsound
detergents. And I came out squelching, unable to find so
much as a towel. Chinaski said not to fuss, the bookies on
the corner was a warm dry place. Chinaski said, Here are
your shoes. He was right.

Flower, Fist & Bestial Wail

Friend of my own up by the bar calling every girl he meets
petal. Some like this guy, some hate his guts, some think
he's sound, some think he's way too much. I owe this gaje;
he's more than bari enough. He's up by the bar, bought me
a drink, a pint, huge welling creamy pint of forgetfulness,
the mouth on him, curiously disengaged from his eyes,
asking about last night, how I got home and with whom -
like that last touch -- with whom. David Hume, ain't no
cause worth talking about, I say at the bar, share a smirk
with myself, because as usual, can't find anything in ma
head about last night or another twisted soul to share ma
humour. That's when I try to tell him about Chinaski,
but he is at the bar, calling a girl there petal. It could go
either way. She's got short cropped hair, heavy boots and
an arts degree on how to talk to your fellow person.
Ma friend with lips like withered rose petals is mouthing
it large and just about to get slapped across the kisser
again.

Strangely, there was ma step-dad fumbling his eyes over
an early edition of the evening paper. He must be out of
work again, shamed on it, hiding in a pub, hoping to meet
someone with a contact, or contact someone, anyone even
... there had to be a job ganning somewhere, with someone
who knew him when he could work like a bull, and
perhaps give him a start, though I notice his bum, looks
like it's given into gravity, it's sliding down the back of his
thighs. He's got his glasses on, he falls and flounders over
the print, looks up from time to time, nurses his pint and
kens that there just has to be someone soon with
something of a job for the man that he used to be not so
very long ago, when he could work like a bull. I could have
gone over, but I had Chinaski, I had ma old friend, with
lips like bust tulips and another pint waiting patiently for
me, provided I wouldn't joke about his lack of luck; I had

all these things and the sight of ma step-father in the next room, not wishing to be humbled by either the present or ma presence. I had all that when I turn to Chinaski who says, flexing the wrinkles in his arms where muscles used to be, who assures us all, Did the jobs no other whites would. We did those jobs. We were the white Niggers. We were the gringo bums, white Hispanics -- we were that strong -- we were that dumb. We were young and we did the jobs no white mother did and we liked it. That's what Chinaski said. The old bull in the corner copped ma reflection in the spotted mirror by the bar, advertising Johnny Walker Red Label, that old bull lowered his paper and ambled out the back, passing the toilet stalls, the fruit-machine and the possible places where someone could have stood, once upon a long time, to offer him a start, because just who he was, back then, sometime, some time good.

There was this long ago when I did what has been called an honest day's work, but not a sobriquet used by me -- not ever. I sat on ma ass, I've sat on ma head, because I did a lot of Gung Fu, so reasonably flexible. I stood in dole queues, in doctors' surgeries ganning mad, troubled in ma superstitions, ma basic physiology, neurology with an idiots guide to anti-social psychology. I sat it out, that honest day's work even when someone was stupid enough to offer it to me on a halter, a slave shackle or some shifty double and the day off for the blobbing on the bru. No matter. I apologised to the vanished reflection of ma step-father, to the stubborn wrinkles in the skin of Chinaski and ma marra buying the round, with his smacked lips, and the dull persistence of a dated phrase -- petal. Call it rosebud, citizen, I mumble to the head on ma pint, acknowledge the fact that I'm work-shy bum, though possessing ma own small pleasures, idiosyncrasies, driven to crass word plays that just don't add up to a hill of beatitudes no more -- ride on, cowboy.

16

With that, with that little lame last noun -- improper -- I launch on the best three cowboy jokes I know, none of `em as amusingly incongruous as the real name of John Wayne. I look at Chinaski, take in the lack of laughter in his reddening eyes and wonder how come he could make the friend I met outside the bookies giggle us an invitation home. For bitterness, I drink the pint of ma horticulturally vociferous friend when he pops off to the bog. How I got any friends left, just don't know: the drunk woman, the man with phatic petals for anyone at all and the crazed dead drunk that is Chinaski.

Find it hard to have friends, I said to Chinaski. Once at a wedding, told a friend that at another wedding I stole twenty quid from his wallet. I did no such thing, not ever, just a badness that came in handy, because I liked the gaje, it was good to see him, that things seemed swell, that he was a good friend and that worried me -- can't cope with folks that like me -- seeing him pissed off, walking away -- it was worth choring twenty quid to me, worth much more. I said this and Chinaski didn't even bat an eyelid, too busy on the floor picking up some good doffs. As ma friend comes back, fighting his zip to order three pints all round without troubling his eyelid for a bat either, leaving me double blinking and incredulous.

Chinaski drinks,

saying nothing,

paying nothing,

and thinks

nothing.

Three-Legged Donkey

Chinaski led the way, betting being one vice I don't have.
It was warm in there, felt the warmth of tired sweat, stale
smoke and a cheap calor gas fire, plum centre in the
middle of the room, safely out of the way of pinned up
races, punters and the queue at the window, where wise
men of the track tottered from time to time to hand over
their money. Gambling, I've no yen for, and I feel smug
about it; felt smug about it back then, warming ma arse
against the fire, steaming: thin stray wisps of steam rising
from ma pants, small pools of discoloured water by ma
pumps: some shoddy baptism into the art of handing ma
money over. Fat lass behind the window with the badly
bleached hair, a strip of mouse-brown sprouting from a
centre parting, vigorous as a squirrel's bush, some kind of
crazy mixed up metaphor, looking cheap and desperate:
those pools of water, leaking from ma battered pumps ran
dye deep.

I didn't see what happened next, but some joker in a faded
sport's jacket was pushing Chinaski around, something
about looking over his shoulder, something about stealing
a tip, probably just something. Not that our Henry
minded, he swung a crumpled left, then another, tried a
flash right and missed and there was hell in there.
The woman with the squirrel's brush in the middle of her
head was shouting her lungs out, threatening to call the
police, to come out there and sort it herself and that no
more bets were to be placed for the one o'clock at...who
cares. She knew her job that woman. A small old man
looking lost and unloved, moved towards the little window
and put on a round robin. Chinaski was in a headlock but
not giving up. Just like the old-time wrestlers on a
Saturday morning, just like a diminutive Dickie Davies
commentary, just like old ladies with handbags and a Phd
in low-cursing: Chinaski stamped on the foot of the man

18

with the faded sport's jacket -- it wasn't anything to do with the Marquis of Queensbury, but it worked. Chinaski was free, celebrated the occasion by head-butting the man of the aforementioned jacket.

Come on, he shouted. Come on, I'll eat your fucking miserable brains, is what Chinaski shouted. The sport's jacket didn't like the sound of the offer, shrugged his shoulders, rearranged his lapels and walked back to his paper and his thoughts for the next available race.

Get out, gob-shite, said the woman behind the glass to Chinaski. I have allus admired northern women's gift of the gab, the cutting phrase, the verbalise of fish-wives -- they gut you with their tongues and then they start. Chinaski blundered out of the dark of the betting shop and he whistled for me as the door swung to like half-hearted saloon doors. Don't come back, you're barred, said Squirrel Nutkin behind the glass. I left that small fire, left it a puddle to dry.

What a first, never been barred from a bookies afore. It was much the same as getting thrown out of anywhere else, besides, I would have much preferred steaming ma arse a bit longer and seeing what the puddles by the side of ma pumps had to say about it all. They looked informative as those ink-blots things that nuts at the psychiatry department dish out. I could just make out the head of a rabbit, a workman warning sign and the opening line from the *Confessions of St Augustin*. I was pished with Chinaski, but I doubt he cared.

We were outside. The rot of leaves blowing about the streets gave everything a scent of melancholy; everything but Chinaski and me who were smelling of death and cheap washing powder respectively.

You put the bet on? said Chinaski. I shook ma head, not even sure if I had the knowledge to do such a thing or not, as I have written rather smugly afore, gambling is not something I had the first clue about, may as well throw your money away as to ask me to sort a bet out. I shook ma head, stamped ma shoe, admired the sleek pump action. Well, what the fuck was you doing in there? said Chinaski. I hadn't an answer for that, looked down at ma pumps, at the slowly forming pools and wondered what it all meant. Chinaski looked at me, he looked like he still wanted answers, that, or pushing ma face through ma arsehole the hard way. Sometimes with Chinaski it's not easy to get along, read the signs and dig your mind for the right words, for something appropriate that could sit alongside a question and answer it to a sufficient degree of satisfaction. Sometimes Chinaski is something of a prick.

I don't know how long we would have sampled the silence out there. I don't have a watch and if I did have a watch I still wouldn't have cared to mark out time that way. But anyway, a friend, an acquaintance of mine, happened along by and gave me something else to think about and something else to do in the day other than come up with something to say for Chinaski. As for himself, he seemed content with the way our travels were headed, he laughed and joked, got invited along on the strength of a dirty laugh.

Chinaski was consoled:

an unplaced bet

burning a hole

through his pocket

yet still joking.

20

Longshots For Broke

Chinaski and I we were outside this bookies, the paint on the door needing sanding off, stripped and repainted. The turf accountants was a dingy, private affair, a small family business, nation of shop-lifters kind of thing. It wasn't owned by William Hill. It was owned by someone who had the relevant licence in the name of E F Benton. It seemed a stolid enough as Gabriel Oak's boots, but it didn't alter the fact that this door needed painting.

Chinaski and I stood outside. There were these diminishing puddles by ma pumps that I bought for something less than eight pound from a cheap shop in the Metro Centre and I had had them for over two years, so wasn't complaining about the way they were prone to let water in or out. They were very democratic pumps when you considered it like that, certainly nay pretentious, snobby designer-ware gear here -- these shoes were open to everything, and you could walk the streets in them without being in fear of losing your life to a foot-fetish mugger. I had grown into them, then out of them. They would flap as I would run for last orders. They would spill the colour of ma socks should I be wearing clothing like that. They told it like it was and when I had nothing but ma skin on, they told it like it wasn't -- they were their very own private verification principle, open textured to experience and probably good for nothing. I liked those shoes, somehow it seemed fitting that my feet would slide about their broken perimeters. Despite it all, they hadn't got long. There was water coming in and out and it was high tide that I bailed out. Chinaski didn't care about shoes. He just wondered what this drunk woman wanted with me. I looked up from the spectre of rainbows smeared, dabbed, into the corners of ma pumped out puddles and knew that it was time I started giving life a bit more attention. Hell, I was shivering out there and still wet behind the ears and toes.

I got a bottle, said the woman, the ageing drunk woman
that I knew, reasonably well, though a stranger she
seemed to Chinaski, which surprised me and, I think, him.
I got a bottle, it's gut-rot, but it's cheap and ma ex-
husband still says to ma mother that he wants me back,
this is what the woman said on the corner of E F Benton's
turf accountants, peeling door and all. It sure beat the
usual, Hi-ya, Now then or Ollreet. And, she did have a
drink on her.

Her place was similar to my place and most of the places
around that part of town. So similar that nothing much
needs to be said just now. Chinaski didn't care for the
details, he was trying to help the drunk woman empty her
bottle, but she was having none of it and not for the first
time.

Bring that tramp along if you must, but if he touches ma
bottle again, I'll break it over his head, said the drunk
woman. Off she staggered, tripped and fell -- Chinaski
shouted, For God's sake watch the bottle! Ma friend,
clutched the drink to her heart, hockled up a spit of a
laugh and thumped the pavement with her free hand in
pure misplaced mirth. You're all heart; a man after ma
own heart. Just the bottle, said Chinaski. Hands off, said
ma friend. Curiously detached from all this, I saw
Chinaski give the bottle and the woman it was attached to
a hand up. I watched them walk off, threatening mutual
grief, sweating laughter and eyes firmly on the drink in
the hand. Stayed at the back, 'cos ma friend was getting
boring the way she went on and on...right inside that
room I was telling you about, bit like ma own, but without
the sick, she was still only just warming to her theme.

I left ma husband for drink. So that bum there definitely
got no right butting in. This she said to me about Chinaski
who then strutted around the tiny maisonette, throwing

out his chest, but more his stomach, thinking he still had what it took to knock a woman around. He looked like some anorexic turkey trying to look good for Christmas, threatening to give someone a good basting.

I felt sorry for Chinaski then, wanted to say something that would smooth things over, make us all feel good and comfortable with one another. I must have tried a good while, 'cos when I stopped I had a glass, a chipped, greasy smeared glass, in ma paw and I was drinking out of it. Chinaski didn't seem to care, he'd taken the only chair in the place and he was trying to read the titles of the books, lined on a single shelf above the bed. I could see his lips move, then, like a deaf man, I tried to read those titles too. Here's a title I got, *There is a time to Cry*. I don't know if there is a title of a book called that or not, yet seeing Chinaski's lips move over something that just might have been those words, I feel sure that there ought to be some book, some slim volume out there for those lips to pick up on. Sometimes, I feel that I'll research this thing properly and dig this book out and when I find that it doesn't exist, I'll write the damn thing masel' and that'll be an end to it all, at last, perhaps.

I was on the bed, I was under the stinking armpit of the drunk. She smelled. I could smell sweat like sour onions stewed in second-hand alcohol. Her breath was bad too, but I wasn't complaining. She had me under her arm, she was filling ma glass with gut-rot and from time to time, when she could remember, she put her left hand down my trousers and started to play with ma cock. You could get mildly happy like this, if your expectations would be small.

I looked at Chinaski's lips again. I don't think what he was mouthing was any kind of book this time: -

Fuck her, you schmuck...

I liked that bit of stranded Yiddish hanging off his smacked-up lips. I liked it so much that I did just that. For a time, I got more than mildly happy, perhaps.

Legs, Hips and Munching Ass

It was like the old joke, I explained to Chinaski. Is sex
dirty? It is if you do it right. I was rimming the arse of the
drunk woman, I was forcing ma tongue into the unholy of
holies and trying to communicate to Chinaski an old tired
joke. He didn't laugh, his eyes gestured get on with it. We
were two stinking people, drunk and lonely with each
other, but up for it. Her head was on the pillow, sometimes
she took it off there to drink straight from the bottle.
I moved ma fingers inside the lips of her arse and she said
to bang `em in. She said she thought that two fingers
would do, but try three for a while and don't try the
whole fist. I did just that, but preferred tongue and
sucking her ass.

All of this seemed like a good idea till I looked down at ma
prick, saw how half-hearted it was with all of this. I bit
her cheeks, I licked her clit, I banged two fingers in and
out of her arse and ma prick just hung there like a hanged
man guilty of death, swinging semi-stiffly from the
tangled gibbet of ma pubes. She twisted round, saw the
problem, bad me to take ma fingers from her body. She
took a swig of wine and came down to ma level to suck
and suckle and tease ma prick into something like action-
stations. Her head was on the pillow again, my fingers
jammed in her arse and she said to put in the prick. Just
born clumsy, I must have been two minutes afore I had
everything lined up and working right. Then it was almost
something good.

Later, when I spat ma spunk inside her body, I can't have
looked like anything but an apprentice contortionist on his
first day. My left hand was hanging on for grim death
around the cup of her left breast, two fingers of ma right
hand had a mountaineer's hold in the crack of the drunk
woman's arse. Ma prick, strangely still pumped up and
jerking, was buried ball deep in her cunt, while the rest of

ma body, fought gravity, seemingly intent on discovering a new advanced yogi position for Meniere's sufferers. Sex -- dirty? Sex is ridiculous. Chinaski was laughing.

I wound things up, a bit of after-play, nibbled her shoulder and she kissed me a mouthful of that wine she bought. She said, Scuse me, then got off the bed and sat on the bog. Her room was so much like mine. There is a curtain that cuts off the all in one bathroom from everything else: a shower, a shitter and small white cabinet for your razor blades and pills. You don't need a sink according to the landlord, you have a sink in the small curtained off kitchen -- this is all rather bijou. Why I am telling you this I don't know, perhaps because this place is so much like ma place.

The drunk woman sat on the shitter, pissed, farted, wiped her arse, wiped her cunt, wiped up and flushed and didn't shut the door. It made sense, those curtain, pull to doors, were good for nothing. She washed her hands in the kitchen sink, so perhaps the landlord had a point. She went back to her bottle by the bed and found it empty, I looked across at Chinaski then, but he just shook his head. Should have been a rumpus then, but the drunk woman had something to say, said, Sex don't make me laugh no more. She said something else too, but I was concentrating on the double negative and thought that it was fine with me. When I stopped playing amateur linguistics, I found her on the edge of the bed, a miserable downbeat pout playing on her face: it came, it went and it allus came back again.

Hey, look at this, I said. For some reason ma prick was still reasonably up. I rolled back on the floor, swung ma legs over ma head and sucked the tip of ma dick -- it was ma party piece, even though I don't get invited to those sort of parties no more. Unravelling masel' I looked up to find that the drunk woman had found this in no ways funny. She said, What's the point of me sucking you, if you can do that, if you can do the job yourself? She said this

26

and I had plenty of answers, but she wasn't interested.
Chinaski had pulled a bottle of cheap wine from his
tattered jacket and she was helping him to pull the cork.
Man, did I feel like some kind of fool and, ma feelings
weren't wrong.

Chinaski and the drunk woman were not laughing. The
drunk woman was explaining to Chinaski about how her
husband kept coming round, pestering her mother with
the notion that he was quite willing to take her back, only
if she gave up the bottle. Chinaski said something smart,
What does that bum want with your drunk mother, when
he could have a drunk you instead? She laughed at that,
she even giggled like a girl, like a drunk slob who had lost
it big -- she howled and through the cheapie laugh she
said, Not mi Mam, me, he wants me back if I give up the
drink. Chinaski sloshed out the drink all round, he
concentrated when he did that, not wanting to lose a drop.
We had us a drink and Chinaski put this proposition to
the drunk woman, Honey, honey, he said, how long does
your husband last when he's on top of you, when he's
acting the stud and thinks you're grateful? Chinaski
asked that and the woman didn't seem to mind. She
answered, she said, Don't know about two to three
minutes flat? Chinaski sort of did a meaningful grunt,
shook his head and then said, How long is a bottle of wine
lasting you? I thought at this point that Chinaski was
getting just a little too personal, but he pushed it and the
woman answered, she said, I guess about fifteen to twenty
minutes. Then for fuck's sakes, said Chinaski, tell that
clown of a husband of yours to leave your mother alone.

The drunk woman laughed, she lay back on the bed,
kicked up her legs and heels and laughed, roared with
mirth, even popped a small gutsy fart out. She said at
last, You I like, you can stay. This she said to Chinaski.
Time I got ma hat, even though I don't wear such a thing.
I said to Chinaski that I would no doubt see him back at
ma gaff. He said move along sonny, I've been wrestling ma
erection for a good half-hour past. I helped masel' to the

exit out, heard their talk, their jibe and grunts all along the corridor. That Chinaski, he sure is a barrel of laughs.

Run with the Haunted

I couldn't complain. I complained all the way home. I'd had a drink, some all right sex, a bit of company eating into the hours of the day that didn't put a smile about ma face. Standing without the drunk woman's room, hearing a drunk bum and drunk bumess laugh and fuck and find some decrepit joy, stung sharper than a first day's urine infection. I was hungry too. Problem with some drunks, they don't eat enough. So okay, I chewed arse, sucked on the glorious porthole of our being as Sammy Beckett would have it and hello sailor, but there was little nourishment there, nothing sustaining not even for a twisted soul like ma own. Suddenly, seeing her dimpled ass, pocked with cerolite -- Christ -- did I want that between two slices of bread and hold the mayo p-lease. I was hungry. I was pished. One bitter fart hating everyone and everything and hating masel' for it. Man that was better, whinging all the way, smacking the pavement with wet dabs of soap-smoked water and things could only reach mediocre.

There was mail on ma doormat, some of it was for me, especially a letter that had arrived three days ago, but I wasn't in the mood for answering ma correspondence, not even the ones with the bright red urgent on them -- who the fuck do people think they are that they can stick an urgent missive into your life -- who's dying? We `re all dying? Who cares? The postman, the mail service, that polite thug who came round last month with a baseball bat and picture of me just to be on the safe side. I didn't care; couldn't care not even when I squeezed ma eyes and tried. I kicked the mail about the place and hoped to see it in hell tomorrow...the mood I was in.

Creeping down the corridor, quiet as a mouse except for the squelch of ma shoes and a raking cough that had come on the week afore and not for shifting. Ma grandma, I think she holds the record; well, some years back she set her heart on having the longest common cold in human history. So far we reckon she's had her current winter's special in excess of three years and counting. I don't see Roy Castle blowing his trumpet about that one -- perhaps there is a merciful God after all. Suppose I shouldn't get green and evil about Chinaski back there fucking the drunk woman and making her laugh. It would have been a lot more misery in ma world if it had been Roy Castle, replete with his tap shoes and trumpet, that had arrived inside ma life this day to share his other-worldly wisdom with me. I don't know -- just the mood...that's all...the mood is all.

Mrs Woodhall. Mrs Sodding Know it All Woodhall. She's there in front of ma door and she's got a black eye and the other one is the evil eye and she wants a word and a pair of dark glasses. I figure this by the way her lips move and some wave of energy washes against these hair-like things inside ma inner ear that have the potential to be deciphered into agro: -

This whole corridor stinks and it's your fault. It smells like someone died in there. It smells like an alehouse pisshouse's wall. It...

It does, I agreed, and not just to shut her up.

Do something about it, she said.

I shall, I lied, pleased that I used the correct first person form.

Ollreet then, I won't report you to the landlord, with that Mrs Woodhall turned and walked back up the corridor towards her own door. Just before she went on in I said ma little piece, I don't know where it came from, but I knew where it was headed. I said, Mrs Woodhall, that black eye you gotten...

What about it?

Does it hurt?

Aye, still smarts a little.

Good, I said and Mrs Woodhall closed her door quietly, firmly. I laughed then, I smiled, I danced and jigged up and down that little corridor singing out loud, Ding dong the witch is dead....etc. It made me laugh and ma smile just got bigger as I leaned against the door jamb of her door and pissed all over her mat. The mat said, Don't forget to wipe your feet. Can you believe the shit people buy. I put ma wrinkled, shrivelled up piece away and opened up ma own door. Christ did it stink in there.

You took your time, said Chinaski, lying on ma bed, smoking a joint, sipping a beer and avoiding last night's puke.

He Caught ma Heart in His Hands
Then He Dropped it Deliberate

You know, you dumb schmuck, that woman right. You ain't
dying, other than the normal dying that everybody living
and not dying is doing -- no illness, no bullet-hole, no
noose around your neck. You not dying, yet you live like
you there already. Just look at this place, this bed even!
Your neighbour has a valid point for once in her miserable
life and you piss on her doormat -- this was quite some
speech from Chinaski and for a while there I thought he
thought he meant it.

I complained, bitched back and we got to argue and bicker
like ancient couples too bone-tired for sex and fit for
nothing else. He threw a pillow at me. I threw it back.
He threw his bottle at me. The bastard made sure he had
drained it first, proved to a nicety that this bum wasn't all
mad. I threw the bottle back, I raced over to the bed to
pummel his head in and slipped on ma own vomit.
Chinaski laughed. He had a point all right. This wasn't
living. Stripping off down to ma skin and skeletal
arrangement I discovered masel' sobbing; sobbing for some
dumb reason that I couldn't be bothered naming and all
I've gotten for comfort is the Late, Great Chinaski.
He's giving me directions like: Get four carrier bags.
Split the piles into sick and dirty, and just dirty. I did that.
Chinaski rolled another joint, lit up, exhaled and helped
me some more. Next stage, split each of the split piles into
light and dark, then bag up with bin liners.

I had a little order in ma life

just like Baa Baa Black Sheep

one bag dark sick

one bag light sick

one bag dark dirty

and one bag

light dirty

and you can't pull

the wool over ma

pig stye.

I got a pen. I wrote the above on the wall above ma bed,
just by the blown-up photograph of ma favourite lurcher.
I wrote it all down, I even signed and dated it. Chinaski
liked that, he sat up, looked up and down, mumbled over
each line and laughed. He slapped me on the back and
said, Boy, you just don't have an original idea in your
head! I had to laugh, that Chinaski, man, what a dark,
light, dirty, sick bundle of laughs.

So, widehead, I said, we gotten fours bags of washing,
big bags too, mindst, now what we do with `em? Chinaski
looked at me as if I was mad, as if never a sane thought
had bothered to trouble ma little, grey, pickled cells. He
looked me up and down like an alien species and gave up.
Eventually his thoughts turned away from stating the
obvious, he said, You got a pop noodle in the house, I'm
hungry here, hadn't a decent bite to eat all day?

He had a point, although I had nothing in ma cupboard,
but some trial box of tea-bags that arrived for somebody
upstairs, some sugar that I didn't take and various little
sachets of shit that allus come buckshee that I never use
at the time but help masel' too for later when I have more
time, but no inclination to use this sort of free
merchandise. Why not, you pay for it anyway by the back-
door. What a woefully inadequate excuse. Crap. Nobody

knows why they take shit like that, that they don't need and don't want, but take just the same. I was one of life's takers: tartare sauce, brown sauce, red sauce, salad cream and mayonnaise: I had salt, pepper and vinegar: I had English Mustard, French, German and wholegrain in a light brown paper packet that made me think of vegans and alternative lifestyles: I had sugar both white and brown. There was something about that sachet of wholegrain mustard that had me thinking about this vegan girl; I was sweet on at one time or another --she was smart, cute and not interested. Don't blame her, though it hurt when she no longer could be bothered with ma work; that hurt the most. Soft-brown sachet of wholegrain mustard -- that went straight in the bin still holding ma regrets, but I still had something of a collection. Suppose, I almost had it all, but I would never use any of it.

Chinaski

What?

Ain't gotten anything.

Oh.

Aye, oh, and what the fuck we gonna do about the washing?

That cheap washeretta on Fifth Ave where the poor go -- we go there -- that's where we go -- that's the place for us -- we the poor, have our own place in the world-

Can it, Chinaski, I got no money.

I thought that had settled it, but I was wrong, Chinaski wandered in then, passed me the remains of his spliff, which I thought was decent, even though these days I don't smoke. So, I sucked on the spliff for good measure and bad memories and got `em both. Chinaski said, You staggered in last night, you threw your wallet and all the change you had in the top drawer.

I did?

You did.

Much left? I asked and there was this small, bright flicker of something that just might have been hope, trying to flare up in the chambers of ma heart. Chinaski stroked his chin, looked concerned about something. Go on, spit it out, I said, that hope thing fainter than ma angina murmur.

Well the situation is, there was a bit left, but I scored some dope, bought some wine, a few bottles of beer, a paper, that sort of thing -- don't reckon they'd be a whole lot left.

I smacked him one. He smacked me back. We were lumping the shit out of one another and it got warm it there. That's when it really smelt bad, had to open the window. It wouldn't open. It was small as a Mormon's ale ration and stuck down with paint from the last time the landlord decorated sometime, around 1973 with this rare shade of orange paint that would have made an Ulster Unionist blush for aesthetic shame. Fuck the window, as I struggled to get some air into ma life, Chinaski bottled me from behind -- so that settled that. There was a crack in ma head, there was blood, warm and viscose sliding down the nape of ma neck, I had four sacks of dirty washing and a dead man that stole ma money. What hurt was the reflection in the mirror, I could see masel' watching masel'; read ma own eyes and everything that they had to say or see. Started to sulk like a child, staring into space while at times, there would shine a persistent gleam of sanity, as sad as a tear ...

`E Glues it together

Hardly a man of the world. Don't get out that often,
struggle sometimes to open the door and even if the door
gets opened, I only manage the step, sit down and watch a
bus pass, but somehow Chinaski got me to the
washerretta on Fifth Ave where the poor go. We had four
bags of washing, very little change, very little anything, no
notes, no credit at the bank and no way to get anything
till next Thursday's dole cheque dived through the
letterbox and onto the communal doormat, ill-fated as an
Icelandic lemming. We were in there, warm and it was
crowded, with no machines of our own. No way out of this
even if you were something of a man of the world. We
were there, world weary and in need of a beer.

We needed a couple of machines even more than a drink.
We had four bags full and no washing machines available.
Was this the end of the industrial revolution as we knew
it? As a bairn, went with ma mother, once, up to the
university to use the launderette there. She wasn't a
student, she cleaned there, and the machines were free or
at least cheap. Ma mother filled two machines, left me
instructions along with a lie, then went home for an hour
or two to get pregnant. If I'd gotten caught ma mother
said to say that ma mother was a mature student
studying for a Phd in Welfare Economics. There was no
one there, but these machines going; for some reason I
started to cry, felt wet through to the skin and bones with
tears. There's no machines available, feel old tears coming
on strong as remembrance of washerettas past.
I'm looking at the big tumble dryers, thinking back to that
time of the lie and the mother and the big dryer there that
I wanted to climb in to and tumble ma tears dry. Inside,
all warm and thrown about like a fairground ride that I
couldn't afford. Kept crying, kept looking at the big up-for-
it dryer, kept feeling tears and temptation, thought it

might be fun to give it a try, climbing inside to dry, and anyway, if I got caught I allus had the lie to fall back on. Sick of tears, I made ma mind up, testing out the biggest industrial tumble dryer for size. There was a snag, I couldn't turn the knob and get inside the dryer all in a one-a. There is such a thing as luck and happenstance and not all of it in19th century fiction: a stranger came in along by, canny too, mindst. So, I asked this young girl in there with a tied-dye t-shirt and no bra, I asked this girl to help for two reasons, at least: first, she was the only other person in there; and secondly, young as I were, I wanted to play, to touch, to fondle if but with ma eyes only, those sweet firm braless boobs of hers. I could not have been ten, but I wanted to fuck that young student. Don't suppose I could put it in those terms, any terms, but ma hairless prick was rock-hard and I couldn't look at the girl's face for the swell of her breasts, snug against this trendy-dyed cheesecloth t-shirt thing. I said, could she help me out, said could she put the money in as I climbed on inside. She thought I was joking, thought that way till I actually climbed inside and wouldn't shift till she put the money in. I did all that and the young girl with the boobs wouldn't laugh no more. She called a porter. I was dragged out, lie or no lie.

Later, when ma mam came back, after I'd done all the washing under the expert eye of the college porter, after all that I did right, including the correct telling of a lie, I got a clout across the face. It stung, we got our bags and we legged it, even as the porter called after us, that he didn't give a toss and not to worry. I got another clout in the beat-up Hillman Imp, first time I'd ever empathised with a chunk of sheet metal. Ma God, ma mother was on form: I got a clout even as we pulled up outside the house. I got a clout, but I couldn't really care. There was something I wanted to do, upstairs alone in the bathroom, all by masel', safe with ma memories. I wanted to pull ma bald, stiff prick as hard as I could. And I did. And a clout didn't come into it.

Chinaski, get in the dryer, I said. For once, he didn't argue. He climbed in, I pulled two twenty pence pieces out of ma back pocket and banged in the money, turned the handle. I laughed like a nut, as Chinaski was battered around and around at top temperature. No one else joined in with ma mirth. They left, left fast, taking their washing howsoever sopping, the smell in there was like pan-fried turd. Chinaski and I had our machines. I let him out. He gave me a clout. We got our washing done. Just like old times. Not quite the best of times.

The Rats

You know, there could have been a chance there, back
there, of the room smelling better despite it all. Chinaski
had pulled that trick with the washing machines, we'd had
a few beers with ma friend and we'd gotten back with
bags of washing that smelt warmly of Proctor and Gamble
products -- something like that, anyway. We got back and
we collapsed, `cos we ain't eaten much, `cos we had to
walk, `cos we were weak already; `cos those four bags took
it out of us. That's the shape we were in when we
staggered in, flinging ourselves on the bed, looking up at
the ceiling, as if we were expecting to see stars shine,
the Lord God of Israel and his heavenly hosts out and
about, stopping off for a picnic on the Milky Way, wings
out-stretched, knocking back the nectar all the way to
oblivion. We looked hard at the ceiling, smelling warm
washing, believing rightly or wrongly that it was smelling
fresher in there, that things were getting better, when I
saw this rat poke its nipple-pink nose out of this hole
where the ceiling met the wall. A rat poked its head out
and it swam down the woodchip wallpaper and into ma
room. Just what I needed, more squatters.

What we do now, I said to Chinaski.

Well, I don't know about you, but I could do with a sleep.

We dozed there for a while, though every so often I would
raise one of ma lids to look across at the rats, nosing their
way through the hole, then swimming down the wall.
I don't know what they did next, just too tired to look or
care, but I was dissatisfied with the whole scenario
somehow, though I couldn't fully explain the reasons for
this feeling. Let's face it, I couldn't explain much. The lid
puckered up, felt heavy, the eye looked about, gave up, just
let the lid slide to a close -- it was time to find some corner

of sleep to dream in. I did just that, waking up later with ma arms round the cold corpse of Chinaski, yet a little refreshed, less weary, nonetheless.

The comfort of sleep.

The comfort of strangers.

Rats in ma bed

And everyone

snoring.

There was a banging of cupboards, Chinaski was up, working his way through all that I had in the kitchen. He found the buckshee stuff and wasn't impressed. He threw the yesterday's second hand tea-bags down the toilet and stuck the kettle on for a brew. A big fat rat ran across the work surfaces, disturbing Chinaski as he tried to light his fag off the hob. You know, you really should sort out these rats, you know that doncha? That rats, they bring plague and disease and nosey enquiries from some sort of health officials, man, if they could see this, you could be in real bother here. You can't live with rats, rats and humans, they don't get along, not even the pet rats. They just stooges, just bits of good feeling, as we force them into their designer cages, make them work their wheels off and nibble bits of cheese off our fingers. They stooges, `cos even they know it ain't like that, that the rest of the rats are either in the gutter or helping the world of science gain useful employment, advance their careers and provide something useful to do for people with feelings to complain and campaign about. These rats, white rats with dumb pink eyes, they look at you and they know. They know if their skin was brown or black and you found them in the bottom of the linen basket, nesting down with young or chewing their way through the week's vegetables that you'd phone somebody quick to come in and sort it,

40

finally. Those clever, weak pink eyes, they know shit, they know lies, they got these whiskers and a keen nose. They can scent bullshit from five hundred yards and up close they clean. They spend more hours in the day washing than you or I. These rats, they've been with us from long ways back and they still here, but I don't think they should be here right now. You know the thing is...

Chinaski babbled on. I was trying to wring a few more ounces of sleep from the balled up bits of wax in ma eyes, gluing ma lashes down, like somehow the whole body know that this waking thing is over-rated. Well, I didn't manage any more sleep that day. The kettle boiled, Chinaski like a gud `un mashed the tea and I wandered through to hear him still lecture on about the frigging rats; rats and fleas, this time giving it large on bubonic plague and Malthusian checks on over-population, possibly moving on to behaviourist psychology and basic game theory. I had all that afore breakfast and for breakfast and if he carried on much longer I'd have to take a carving knife out of the drawer, and slit his throat. That Chinaski, man at times, he's such a bore.

Can it, for fuck's sakes, can it.

Silence,

quiet as a

mouse.

I slurped tea and Chinaski smoked, saying nothing now, pretending not to sulk, pretending that his feelings, such as they were, weren't hurt. He did that for a whole five minutes. It hurt. He couldn't cope, banging down his chipped mug, he said, So just what do you plan to do about the rats?

That's it! That's it you furry fuckers, you cunts with the

long fucking tails, you fucking come on out. Come on then, vermin! I was screeching, I was taking a knife from the kitchen drawer, then hunting around the room, that small rectangle of kitchen, cruel as a farmer's wife -- Nimrod the nutter armed with a butter knife, plastic handle, slightly melted at the top. I ripped open cupboards, draws when out fell a box of new white candles that I'd forgotten about.

Chinaski!

What you want?

See this.

I'd opened the cupboard underneath the sink. There was a rat that scurried off quick, that ain't the point, point was this: there was a mound of stored up rice in the corner. These rats had been stealing rice, maybe from Ralph Singh, who moved in about a month back, lived in the flat above. What the hell, me and Chinaski couldn't give a toss. We hugged each other, we capered and danced some sort of two man pavanne. We washed up some rice, boiled it up. We had breakfast, Chinaski even put a little sachet of red sauce on his. No feast but no hunger.

We were happy. Chinaski asked if he could borrow ma pen, write up a poem in praise of rats up by ma own work near the picture of the lurcher while I did the washing up. I told him to get fucked -- if I didn't have an original idea in ma head, at least ma scrawls on ma walls were ma very own. But, we were happy, we had us a store of food at last. And them rats, them rats could stay for us. Long as they like. Buckshee. Giving it rice. Rent free.

The Community Backyard

I gave all ma money to Chinaski, why not. He'd `ve stole it
anyway, none of that, can I borrow a few cents
while....shit. That Chinaski stole it all, but he never told
me lies. He was allus fair with me like that. He'd say, Hey,
that five pound note you scrunched up small put between
your big toe and its neighbour on your left foot, the foot
with the three socks on, with the `lastic band on top, you
know that scrunched up fiver I'm talking about...Well,
that five pound note, sanctioned by your Queen of
England is the very same promissory note that I put on a
horse and the horse it didn't win. It didn't come close.
It was half a mile back, trotting round like this was
vacation day. Doncha get pished with me, boy, it's that
horse you want to consider having words with. I'm only
telling you this, `cos I feel for you, every time you go off
the wall thinking you got money and you ain't, that you've
got money tucked away safe and you ain't, that there is
two pounds of change hidden in a tin, wrapped up in
cellophane, a plastic bag, stashed in the toilet reservoir,
I feel for you the way you tear around the house looking
for all the money you don't have, the way you bang your
thick head against the wall and holler like a minstrel
black, like what the Southern White still call Niggers -- it
beats me up, the way you go cartoon-niggerish, rolling
your eyes, pleading up at heaven, whupping yourself, for
money you don't have, probably never had or never will
have. So to save you all this disgrace, all this mental
anguish, I'm taking care of your money and if you want to
talk to someone about this, if there is no money for our
joint account, or money for booze or some food, I want you
to know that it ain't ma fault, so doncha go wanting words
with me about any of all this, you hear? Go talk to that
horse, get it off your chest, tell that slow, sorry, four legged
mother-fucker just how broke we is. Do that, do just that,

but don't look for what ain't there, can't bear to see you mad, mad and broke and beating yourself up -- it's no joke-

Shut it will you, Chinaski, change the record, take ma money, but just shut it for once.

Chinaski never told me lies. He stole ma money. He screwed ma girlfriend while I slept. He took the piss out of everything I wrote, but he never mistreated me to a lie. He had more respect for himself than that. I wasn't worth a lie. I wasn't worth anything, Chinaski stole all ma money, such as it was...aye, such as it was.

We were out the back, sitting in that moist fall's sun. We had us a pot of some cheap sweat-shop brand, from which we took two ex-jam pots of brimming tea, without milk, without sugar, without handles, `cos we broke the cups and mugs and things like that during some argument the night afore. Well, I think things got a tadge too hot when I said that Carver was a better writer than he was; more, that Ray was a damn sight better person too -- he'd beat his demon, he got to the gravy boat at last and ma only sorrow was he didn't get chance to savour for longer its good juice. That was some argument, even the Woodhalls stopped their tea-time pitch battle to listen and laugh for a good half hour, but then they were back to their own problems...still, I don't regret saying that to Chinaski, not after he smacked me in the teeth with ma favourite mug.

So, back to those jam jars, what could we care, there was plenty of rice that the rats were bringing in, I had clean washing for once, and I suspected things weren't too bad, that somewhere in the folds of pockets, in the linings of Chinaski's wear, there was some change still from what he did down at that washeretta where the poor people go.

Folk in there they left when Chinaski was sweating it and hotting up, rolling inside that drum of that drier. They left us with all the machines in the place technically open to us but for the want of change in our pockets. We felt like kings, but both of us secretly were republicans and by that I mean we thought the French had the right idea some centuries back. We sat in our little kingdom and Chinaski explained about the bad old days, how they could fix your shoes, fix your car, fix your...I don't know. I stopped listening after a while, he was getting on the wrong side of boring, that and he was sitting on ma left side and ma ear don't work so good on that side of ma head, old labouring injury from when I once went to work. I stopped listening, but not looking. There was Chinaski, he'd taken his shoe off and that stink just got richer by half a tonne of rotten Roquefort and stinking Stilton. I was almost used to this, breathed in quick and deep, best way to get rid of a bad smell -- brain gets piss-bored of sensing it.

Chinaski half-limped, lopsided like, all the way to the nearest machine. He got his liberated shoe in one hand and he sort of smacked the machine in the right place. He rifled around for a bit and the machine was knackered, there was change in his hand and the machine was open to offers, run any cycle, do anything you wanted it to do in its line of business, and potential operational functionality. I was impressed. Chinaski did `em all, gave me some change to hold, as he sorted out the four bags full. Those bags with the sick, they even got a pre wash; generous like that was Chinaski. Loved the guy.

We got our washing done.

I got to hold some money.

Chinaski put his shoe back on.

Had me some clean washing.

Chinaski never lied to me.

And I wanted to shoot a horse.

Cold Dogs

Cold as January, rime crisp spunk over the bedspread,
wished like hell someone else was there. I had Chinaski
but he was as cold as a graveyard dog. We were shivering,
we were holding on to one another, praying hard that the
whole damn world would slide off down to hell...at least
for the winter. I was thinking about ma girl, if she was ma
girl or not, and even if not, would she still like to call and
have some disappointing sex with me. I was thinking
about that girl and I hated that uniform she was wearing:
I wanted to rip that damn
`service/upstairs/downstairs/retro-30s shit right off her
back, strip her down to just the sweet thing she is -- I had
mixed intentions, not all of `em good.

Chinaski said, Give the girl a key for Christ's sakes.

What she want a key for? I said, she don't call that often.

Chinaski said, You got a couple of spare keys?

Aye, I've got loads of spare keys, practically cut a new set
every month, sometimes twice a month -- guess I've got
loads of spare keys scattered all over the universe, I said.
Spare keys I have, just not on me.

Chinaski said, You know that old tin of *Uncle Joe's Mint
Balls*. You know the tin I mean, just by that Chinky
broadsword you don't practise with no more. Say wasn't it
a present from a friend.

It was, I said, a good friend, so good, in fact, heard jack
shit from him in the last ten years.

Chinaski said, Stop whining. Inside that tin, you once put
your keys. You were drunk, you told yourself not to forget

in the morning. But you forgot. In fact, you did the same damn thing three nights later and you forgot about it all. In fact, if you really want to know, you did it again about four or five nights ago and you still damn well forgot. You're a consistent drunk.

Stuff your facts and in facts and forgets, I said, stuff `em up your ass.

Chinaski laughed.

I got on ma hands and knees and wandered around the perimeter of the bed, feeling for ma broadsword case. I found it, all covered in dust and neglect, got ashamed of masel' all over again. Time to get back with the plan, train, be fit, work out, work, write, live, play, reggae, put the wireless on 3 and skank along to a Schoenberg concert -- the good, bad old days, when I was just as miserable but a damn sight fitter with it. I found the box case that had ma sword in it, next I found the tin with three sets of keys for safe-keeping. By the bed, I stood, keys balled in ma fist, lost in thought, stood lost, wondering how to unlock this frozen moment.

What am I doing now?

You are getting your good, clean gear on and we go into town and we call on your girl and we give her the God damn set of keys. We say, here, take your pick, babe, and she takes a spare set and she can call in on us, whenever she likes, even when we not in.

What?

Doncha what me, boy, think about it. We go out, no key and your woman she call and she goes again, maybe she finds someone who is in.

Hadderway, man, and shite.

Colourful, but listen up. She calls round, we not in, she let's herself in, strips off warms, up the bed, and we come in and we have us a good time.

Who's this us and we, all of a time, all of sudden.

What the hell, I've had more ass and better ass than you've ever had, including your wet dreams, brother. So come on, get on the good, gear, doncha go shame your girl like that, some place she working, remember?

I got dressed, did ma hair, unknotted all those mad curly locks. I looked good...Well, I looked good, if I'd been some Mick folk singer back in the seventies working the folk festivals with Frankenstein revived ballads and hate chill as a pint of Guinness for the English. I looked that good, but it was all I had, that and Chinaski at the door wanting out, like some cat eager to crap on your neighbour's lawn.

Hold on, a minute, I said, there's a problem.

Chinaski said, What gives.

I sat on the edge of ma bed, ma tousled mazzard, all folk curls, leather flagons, warble in the back of the throat, scent of roll-ups and that oil that I can never remember what it's called. Edge of the bed, head in ma hands, despair sitting like a newly hired succubus on ma rounded shoulder. Depression coming on, rocking back and forth, moaning with the blues and cold, `cos I've only a thin silk shirt on, with a burn at the back, tucked into ma moleskin trews.

Chinaski said, Now what's up?

Nay money, I said, just nay money, man, it's expensive in there, a cup of coffee is a five quid affair.

Chinaski said, Don't have an affair.

48

Ain't funny, I said.

Chinaski laughed and put a whole bunch of loose change
on the bed. Some of it was pound coins, two of it was two
pound coins and a couple of fifty pence pieces.

Where the hell did you reave this from this time? I said,
though thankful just the same.

Some from that place we took the clothes, some from that
tin of *Uncle Joe's Mint Balls*. You've a habit of putting
change in there too. Dincha look?

I shook ma head, stuffed change in ma pocket, rattled it
like ma grandmother's false teeth that she'd leave in a
glass in the kitchen overnight, (it stops her talking in bed)
shook change just like that, `cos we had enough for
another bite out of life. Looked up at the great Henry
Chinaski, felt suddenly sad, unsure how long I was due to
have a friend like that. Maybe all this was borrowed time,
overdue, pay the fine and do not pass go.

You know, I said, you know, Chinaski, you is the only
friend I have.

Chinaski said, I ain't never no friend of yours.

I laughed, Chinaski laughed and the neighbours banged
on the adjoining wall again to complain about the noise.

I don't love ma neighbour.

I don't covet her ass.

Crucified in a Handshake

I was looking for places to put clean washing, a hard thing
to do in a room that size, with the dirty variety it don't
matter a damn, but clean stuff, especially given all that
trouble that Chinaski went to, well that washing, still
slightly warm and chemically fragrant, that washing
deserved better. I went around that bedsit/maisonette and
I searched high and low for somewhere to put that
washing. Porn mags, there were some porn mags left by
the previous occupant of that room and many of the pages
were spunk-glued together. I know this, because Chinaski
told me about them. As I was rifling through this old chest
of drawers, harling out junk, dust and smut, Chinaski was
behind me, curious. He took the mags went over to the
bed. He looked them over like a connoisseur. He thought
them tame. He thought them bland. He thought that the
best pictures had been ruined already. No stopping him,
I was cleaning out drawers hoping for a hand, but
Chinaski was on a mission. He divided the spoilt from the
indecent and he made a tidy job of it. The cum-whacked
rejects got the bin, that bust bin by the bed, falling apart,
partly chewed by rats and bursting at the side with ma
crusty tissues, crunched up with wasted seed -- that bin
was almost, verily biblical in its futility of issue wasted
tissue. That bin got full after a while, not that I cared I
was wiping out drawers to put in ma clean stuff.

Here, have this, said Chinaski. He passed me a blond with
big floppy breasts like bloodhounds' ears and her gash
spread wide open for eye-fucking. Could see the clit, that
little bud of pleasure, could see the ragged, mouse-ear of
her vaginal opening, could see where she'd inexpertly
shaved around her mound, getting rid of the excess,
leaving nothing put a flimsy triangle of twisted pubes the
colour of wet sand. You could see all that but not for long.
I lined the drawers then verily covered that woman with

clean socks, boxer shorts and t-shirts that I used like vests. Chinaski passed me other adult material to line the rest of the drawers. Not a big fan of porno but couldn't help getting a chubby on. Chinaski the connoisseur was way beyond me, getting near to completing his second session of slapping the salami and that poor bin of mine was overflowing. I could have joined him, but there was a ring for ma room -- the bell went. That don't happen often, so I rushed out, hoping it wasn't a mistake, some other resident forgetting or losing their key; doubted this, as normally I'm the one without and without the key, knocking someone up to bad mouth me at three in the morning, `cos they're up early for work in the morning and I'm steaming and it's the third time this week -- Go boil your head, I shout, push past them and find, thankfuckfully that I hadn't bothered to lock ma door, whisper ma thanks goodnight to the one I've woken, get told to fuck off and flop into ma bed, quiet as the well-paid dead.

But anyways, I was on the inside opening up the front door to find the person who used to be, perhaps, probably still is, ma girlfriend in her work things, her dull brown waitress uniform from that posh coffee shop in town. There was someone who might be someone to love on ma doorstep, wanting in and I'm hoping that Chinaski has finished using the bed, the pornographic material afore we get back inside the room. Chinaski, what a gentleman, he's put the rest of ma clothes away, and keeping out of the way, slouched up in the kitchen against the sink, having a cup of weak tea, though prefers coffee, trying to roll six doffs together into one semi-decent smoke, leaving me and the girl some quality time together.

Can't stop, got to meet Mam at Aldi for the shopping, getting a taxi back. Just popped in, two things, your marra, the one that says petal, he's in the Spread early, says to come along down, he'd stand you a drink. Other thing called in for, what we gonna do about us? She said this, put her bag and her coat down on the dressing table, looked me up and down, looked at the porno crap in the bin and the spent tissues and I knew she didn't approve, thought she'd start lecturing again, but she just repeated the question.

Don't know, I sort of Valium-drawled. I love you, allus love, you walk away now and there's pieces of you cluttering ma head and heart still, but...

But what?

But I don't know if I can do you any good...deep down, you deserve better than this.

You got a point. It's corny, but you have a point and I have no time. She said this, this cute frown about her face, as she took her from her body a coffee-cream blouse and white bra. She ditched the frown too, laid back on the bed. An't got much time, wank over ma tits.

I put ma knee between her legs, nuzzled up to her pants, nice and snug, slid ma left hand between knee and pants, rubbed ma fingers inside her pants, looked at the soft light laying on her breasts and curiously dark nipples. Frigged quick, pulled it hard and squirted a fine, globbing jet of spunk. Felt that ejaculation way down, almost hurt ma balls, felt it thudding down the stalk of ma prick all the way to the base of ma arse -- almost sick with how good it was.

Rub it in, she said.

I rubbed it in, hands oiled up with juice, drying it out of her breasts, her soft belly, rubbing down to the side, up, back up to her breasts, fondled, kneaded, stroked, then tweaked her nipples.

Bite `em, she said.

I bit them.

Now get off me, gotta meet mi Mam.

I walked her to the door, we didn't kiss goodbye, nothing seemed decided and she left. She left me there to watch her walk off in the rain, wearing her waitress uniform from that posh cafe in town. It all hurt. It all hurt as someone had walked up the path unnoticed, someone else getting into ma small, quiet sorrow, but this joker wanted to talk about God. I told him where to stick his free copy of *Watchtower*. It wasn't original and I guess the man had heard it and its ilk many times afore, 'cos it didn't stop him bellowing as I tried to shut the door, I'll pray for you ma brother.

Had enough, I kicked the door back open, pulled him back with the strap of his brown satchel and promised him there and then, that if he ever prayed for me, I'd rip his fucking lips off.

Let him go, said Chinaski.

I let him go but said to Chinaski, Why? Why let that smug, self-righteous-

Can it for Christ's sakes, let's go and get that free drink off that friend of yours.

We did. We did just that and I don't think that a stranger prayed for me. Hope not, had a pretty full schedule of revenge ahead already -- there was still a horse to have a word with, maybe shoot, let alone take the lips off one of God's door to door salespeople. It's a full life being mean-hearted.

Enough Confessions of an Insane Beast

So we had a bottle of vodka, so I can't quite remember
how we got it either, but none of any of this debarred the
drinking of it. Me and Chinaski we stole some lemons, a
bar of soap and a white plastic container of table salt that
had had something done to it to make it free-running.
Liked the sound of that -- free running. I distinctly
remembered stealing the goods, `cos this old woman on
the tills, all bulldogs jowls and hairy top lip, this jobs-
worthy, said, Put it back, lad, I've seen you, we've all seen
you, you're on camera, y' soft bugger -- put it back.

I wouldn't, though, said to Chinaski to act like we an't
heard or if we had, that we thought that the woman on
the till wasn't even talking to us. Told Chinaski not to
worry, I had the goods.

The woman on the till I think was losing her patience. She
said, Son, put it all back please, the cop shop is just over
the road. And that jacket, that big jacket with all those
big, deep inside pockets, that jacket that you are using to
hide your stash -- you're not frigging wearing it, lad.

That woman on the till had a point. Suddenly I looked
down. I was wearing odd socks again, ma Tom and Gerry
Hogarth-like boxer shorts and a pale green t-shirt that
once upon a time had more zest and colour in it. That kind
woman on the till had a point. What she didn't have was
Chinaski hitting a super sob story, straight from the front
line of professional charity pitches. It made me cry, the
language he used, he was on about some sad case, no
money, a rat-den where he lived, that no one loved
him...man, there was more, but I was weeping already. I
said to Chinaski, For the love of the Yid Jesus take him
these things, that charva needs them more than I.
Chinaski took them in his arms, then whispering low, he

explained to me on the way out, that I was the subject of his rare barn-storming soliloquy. Felt insulted then, but too busy to bitch as we were walking past the woman on the till and she still didn't seem happy, not that she dared to stop Chinaski. The man on a mission.

So we got this bottle of vodka and we drinking with panache. There's a ritual going on. You sacrifice a virgin, kiss the ass of the devil and get bum-fucked by a goat. There probably is a ritual like that somewhere along the line, but it wasn't the one we were on with. The next day, I wished it had been. What we was doing instead was, licking a bar of soap, taking a pinch of salt, biting on a slice of lemon then downing a big shot of vodka. I said to Chinaski, Ain't you supposed to do something like this with tequila or something?

No way, said Chinaski, I wouldn't waste good tequila on a bar of soap like this. I wouldn't waste water on a soap this raw, what you pay for it?

Henry, Henry you nicked it.

That's awright then, said Chinaski, and we licked the soap, pinched the salt, bit the lemon and drank. We got wasted, so rotten drunk we puked up bubbles. Chinaski gotten foaming so bad I thought he had rabies and was gonna rush out and bite a dog.

Just afore ma final puke, just a few minutes afore I passed out inside the toilet bowl, clinging on to the bog-brush for dear life, I got to remember where we got the bottle of vodka from. It didn't seem to matter then. It mattered not to Chinaski, he struggled through the doorway, blind-foaming drunk and pished all over ma head without noticing. Darkness was coming for me, too drunk to care, too wasted to bother having words with the blackguard, so Chinaski pulled the light on and on seeing me, sort of apologised for what he done. He felt so bad, he lurched back to the bedroom for the soap. He washed me up. He really washed me up. He even rinsed me down too, no three times, despite it taking a long time for that cistern to fill. I was losing the light again, no tunnel opening up for me to receive ma immoral soul, sound of angels, quiet calm... None of that: Chinaski put a pillow under ma head, turned off the light and washed his hands of me. Black. Just black. Said to Chinaski was death like that. Shouting from ma bed, he said, not so melodramatic, death comes in cheap Technicolor these days. And with that he wished me a silent goodnight.

Goodnight, Henry

Goodnight, Chinaski

Goodnight, ma friend

Goodnight, ma ald mukka

Goodnight, ma khustaigh charva

Goodnight, ma bari gaje

Fucking hell, it's not the fucking Waltons in there, said the wifey from next door, banging on the walls and hollering at the top of her lungs.

Goodnight, Mrs Goodhall.

Goodnight, son.

White Legs and Thighs

We weren't drunk, of that I insist upon. It's not much to stand firm on, but it's a start. We were shaking. The drink from The Spread with ma mate had gone not to our heads, but our whole bodies, seemingly. Outside, the night drawing in, rain, not cold, but rain, running against your body, chilling you, shramming you, leaving you shaking on the step, fumbling with keys, numb from the neck down. It took three attempts, some cursing, a smatter of bitter laughter, afore we got the door open. I flicked the three - second light. It is more than that, but given that the landlord pays for this light, the light don't last long. I flicked on that light, nearly died. There was Mrs Woodhall on her hands and knees, wearing a rather faded night gown and curlers in her hair. Her face was removed of its customary make-up, strangely enough she looked younger, but could have been the drink. Younger/older what the hell, gave us quite a shock, not something you expect to see when shaking with beers.

Thought it was you, fumbling with the door again. Why don't you lay off it, said Mrs Woodhall.

I was desperate to say something crude and witty, but nothing would come to mind but, Go and put on some fish-fingers. That didn't make sense, besides I was still shaking, had rain in ma bones, dripping like manic marimbas. Instead, the best I could come up with, even after staggering down the hallway to ma door none to quickly was this, What you doing, Mrs Woodhall?

How many times do I have to tell you, lad, that ma name is Mrs Goodhall, she said, looking up from down on her knees with a scrubbing brush in both hands, looking like something from a period drama.

Well, anyway, Mrs, whatcha doing? I said, holding on to
ma door handle, playing the *Golden Shot* with ma door
key as Chinaski comes out with that old Bessie Smith
number, You got the right key but the wrong key-hole.
I allus found that more than a lot ambiguous. There's
plenty of meanings out there, but the one that sticks in
ma smutty mind is that maybe the subject of the song had
slipped up with his tool. It's easily done. One time this girl
in the Smoke, we getting it on, smoking hash most of the
day, drinking a little, it hot and sweaty down there.
Ma prick's leaking semen, she juiced up and we go for it,
a tad awkward, slip down a bit then I'm in. Poor girl
mumbles to me, Wrong hole, you're up ma shitter. Swear
blind I didn't know, asked her if she wanted me to remove
it, she was some sport, said she'd try it for a change as if
ganning for a mocha rather than a cappuccino.

What do you mean what am I doing? said Mrs Woodhall,
from the floor, from her knees, a suddy scrubbing brush in
her hands. What's it look like I'm doing, lad?

I didn't answer, I'd found ma keyhole with ma key and
I was no longer thinking of Bessie Smith and triple or
quadruple entendres. Mrs Woodhall, though was not
through, she said, I'm scrubbing this corridor, because it
stinks of piss.

She said `piss' very sibilantly, like a snake, an angry
anthropomorphic snake with possible loose-fitting teeth --
said it with venom. Just afore stumbling through ma
doorway, I decided to say goodnight, but came out with
something different instead, just for variety, Well, Mrs
Woodhall, I guess those cats of yours will just have to go,
if they carry on messing in here like that.

It ain't the cats, piss-artist and the name's Goodhall.

Night, Mrs Woodhall.

Night, Son.

All of damn sudden, feeling blue, perhaps ma neighbour was a good person after all. You know, bent down there scrubbing floors is no life. I could see her thighs, her creamy white thighs, still firm, good and strong, light patchwork, tracery of green to blue veins, like some kind of cheese, perhaps. That split in that old faded dressing gown, riding up, shewing her thighs, that split hinging flesh had me thinking. What was her old man doing fucking around with bits of kids when he could have those big beautiful thighs around his necks, could suck that honey-pot every night, instead of trying to reinvent his youth out there -- that paper-girl, fifteen, a hard case, met her down at the clap clinic already, heard she had an abortion too, puts it around -- none of ma business -- don't know who I am feeling sorry for, those beautiful thighs -- I'd like to stroke `em, slow and sensuous, I'd like to give them a bit of a nibble, a little lick then in to kiss her sweet cunt...Shit, there were tears in ma eyes for an aging woman, on her hands and knees, scrubbing some drunk's piss from her door.

What you reckon, Chinaski?

I reckon we have a cup of tea, we're shaking, this could be a cold; if we get a cold as we go into winter we won't see the spring.

Chinaski?

What?

You bothered about seeing the spring?

Nope.

Me neither.

Chinaski made tea, we cupped it in our hands, slept in our wet clothes, heard the rats bitch about how much rice we'd took.

Outside, in the hall

with the lights out

a woman stops scrubbing,

the floor wet, she hoping

soon her man will

come along in

to break his neck.

Never been to Armentieres
No M'am
Never

I want to warn you about something, said Chinaski. I could tell he was going to go off on one, something had been brewing all day, ever since that tramp laid into that priest and all the grief that brought us, but mainly me. I could tell that Chinaski had his soap box out, but I still tried to sit it out in stupefied nonchalance. It was late, early morning, we hadn't been to bed for two days, a milk float, eased itself into the night, all rattling bottles and dull thud of diesel engine. I had a smoke, not a big smoke. I like ma mix with plenty of grass, bit of hash, not too much baccy. That's the way I rolled it, small, but strong with Ol' Nick Nicotine kept to an incendiary necessary minimum. I was smoking, but not a lot, as the late Paul Daniels would have had it. Chinaski had a big bird of a smoke going; nicotine in there was enough to kill a whole Jesuit seminary. It was a smoke and he smoked it well. Still, Chinaski had something on his mind and despite ma lack of interest in his tub-thumping, he continued just the same. What I want to tell you, said Chinaski, is that if you ever get rich, or even awright, you get so you can fill your belly, wear the sort of clothes you want to wear, have yourself a holiday, treat your woman and the kids, perhaps you get to own your own home even, all that stuff ...you know what I'm saying?

I do, I said, and did.

Well, you ever get rich like that I don't want you to forget none how much poverty hurts... Hurts so ...You hear me -- doncha forget.

I just nodded. I didn't say no more and neither did Chinaski for a while. Couldn't help thinking of all the meals I'd missed, all the clothes I hadn't worn, holidays year in/year out never had, the shit heaps of places where I lived, what I'd done to put some kind of money in ma pocket, thinking about all the love I'd wanted and craved, how I would have liked to have bairns, watch `em grow up, take `em down to a park, give `em advice how not to end up broke and old and bitter as a cleric's turd, had all this in ma mind and the remains of a smoke, smoldering ma fingers so yellow brown it felt like I was a corpse already: abiotic as sun-cured bananas, but a lot less esculent.

Hadn't planned on it, but I rolled another smoke, just the same. I lit, inhaled, wondered what to scrub ma fingers with, heard pile ointment was good for some things, heard about models using it, but couldn't remember if it was for grass stains in their digits. Doing all this, but all I was doing was avoiding paying attention to Chinaski. It didn't last. I said, Hey, Henry, don't worry, don't ever want you to worry about the hurting, about forgetting that hurt you have, you live, eat and breathe when you poor. You don't worry, `cos I'm never going to be rich.

Shit, I know that, but it was the only bit of advice I had and I'm leaving you in the morning, had to leave you something, what with you sharing what you had, giving me a place to crash these last couple of weeks or so.

You ain't going. You can't go. You all I have barring the rats.

What you mean, your girlfriend has her own key.

Aye, but she in't coming back -- is she?

Nope, said Chinaski, it was the nearest I'd seen him to blushing. And so he fucking should.

So why you're leaving?

Well, you said to -

I know, I said that then, but you stayed and you can't leave me now.

You sure.

Course I'm sure, I said.

Well, guess I'll stay a bit longer then, guess I do that after all, said Chinaski, sitting back against the headrest of the bed, puffing on his smoke like a contented, massacred Native American.

I lay back too, smoked ma new smoke, felt sorry, black-blue, deepest blue sorry, for everything that had ever happened to the Native peoples of the Americas. I also felt bad for saying what I had said, felt real pissed off that Chinaski was staying on after all the harm he'd done. Not that it mattered, we lay back against the headrest and we smoked our own individual spliffs of peace.

Big Time Fling

I couldn't help thinking that perhaps I ought to have a tin whistle or a fiddle case or a finger in one ear or something. I was in ma best clobber, Chinaski had tried to do something with ma hair and I still looked like a third rate Padaidh on the folk circuit: two songs in very bad Gaedhlig and a score of Dylan covers and an Oirish Granmammy somewhere in the cupboard alongside the skeletons. That's what I looked like, looked like a disgrace, or a proper caution as ma Grandma would have it, nay wonder that ma girl blushed me a sunset as Chinaski and me came through the door, took a seat not too far from that mini grand, then tried to order a coffee in that posh café of hers -- no wonder at all, ma sweet girl blushed, you could have fried sardines on ma cheeks, red as a Cardinal's bum. We was waiting there a while, like embarrassed punters at an over-worked brothel, afore ma girl would come over. I loved the way she walked, she walked strong, didn't mince, no too girly-girly, but some solid young woman, bruising ma way, her breasts filling out her top, her soft belly, lipping over just a bit that skirt she wearing, the way she walk, some brush of colour in her cheeks, and stray wisps and bits of hair, fighting to get free, falling about the sides of her face in soft, gold curls. Man, I don't even like blondes, much prefer ... never mind what I prefer, but that plump, young woman, fair and blond and happy and walking over to me. That girl was doing ma heart good. If she'd said, Take our your heart and eat it, I'd have said, Pass the salt.

What in fact she did say was this, What the cunting fuck you doing here? You say you got no money, that we can't afford to go out, do anything, and you walk in the most expensive, rip-off tourist place in town -- eh, fuckwit!

There was nothing I could say to that, though Chinaski

whispered, Give her the keys. Sorry, babe, I said, found these keys, spare, found a bit of brass, thought you'd like a set of keys...thought...

She smiled. Her teeth could have probably done with a scrape and polish, but what was that to me. She took ma keys, said, Wait there. We waited, Chinaski and I, looking out of place, by a mini grand piano while the tourists ate well, thought what a nice place it was and talked to each other in accents I couldn't afford and don't regard. We didn't mind, ma sweet-sweet woman was back, walking towards me balancing a coffee pot on a tray that had a fine coffee mug and a medium curd tart. She put it down on ma table, did that sort of whisper in ma ear that normally went something like, Is everything satisfactory, Sir? What she said was this, Haven't washed your cum off ma tits, yet, still wearing you, babe. She stuck her tongue in ma ear and waltzed away, her hips shaking the blood right down to ma balls and beyond. Swear, If I'd died then, I would have died a more than happy with ma share of misery.

There was a racket playing, didn't notice it at first. But someone was playing the piano and singing. It was an old tune, an old song. It was Chinaski doing a good impression of a bad Tom Waits, felt for sure that we'd be shewn the door, but nobody minded, nobody heard, some even clapped as later, without paying, we walked out the door.

Above the street lights and lit up monuments a cow-moon was blazing, tried to howl like a wolf, nothing came up but a ball of phlegm spat into the gutter, but Chinaski knew what I meant, he said, Come along, let's get along home. When he said that, for once I thought that with ma girl having a set of keys to ma bedsit, that I had at last somewhere to call by that name.

Chinaski said, You nothing but a sentimental fool:

your place should be condemned

it wet and it's cold

there's mould growing up the walls

water coming up through the floors

there's rats and fleas and that smell off the drains

the hallways stinks of piss

you behind with your rent

no food in you larder

no paper to wipe your ass

your money is spent

the lights go out when it rains

you got bronchitis and bed sores

you-

You go on too much, Chinaski.

It's all I've got, it's home,

so what's eating you?

It's ma home too,

said Henry Chinaski.

Bakers, Bakerman, Bake Me a Cake

Chinaski and I we were coming along back from the clap clinic and it was raining. We passed a bakery. It had everything in it, both sweet and savoury. Felt good hanging outside, felt as covetous as dirty old men around a porno store, just on the sniff, just looking. Chinaski said, What you got. I told him that I had eight-two pence only: I had this sum in the following denominations of coin of the realm: one fifty pence, one twenty pence, one ten pence and one two pence, bent and dinted at the edges. Chinaski said, if you're holding back on me, I'm gonna kick your butt all down the street. I said to Chinaski that if he found any more money on me, then I'd gladly have ma butt kicked all down the street, in fact, if I think I'm still supple enough, I'll kick ma own butt down the street. Chinaski said, Hands up. So I put ma hands up and he pulled out the coins, one by one, adding them up and suddenly there was this small, wee extra, shiny five pence piece in there, in with the rest and the fluff and an old screwed up bus ticket. Well that was it. Chinaski kicked ma butt all down the street, when he got tired I helped him out a little and did this fancy Gung Fu manoeuvre, bit like stepping into quintessential stance, whatever. When ma friend Chinaski got tired, I helped him out and kicked ma own butt. All for an extra five pence, which, later, Chinaski confessed, he'd planted himself.

How we laughed.

We were on another street. We were on our way home from the clap clinic, we were nearing our own bake-house, where they sold yesterday's bread for a lot less than half-price, I pretended it was for ma crippled dog...I think I had a dog, think that was the lie I told. I know they never believed a word, just thought I was poor scum, having it cheap and trying to cover up about it. Didn't rightly care

what they thought, though, strangely, caring enough to lie
in the first place. That was the direction we were walking
in down this road, back from the clinic and up ahead,
midway on this street, all gaudy red and yellows was a
porn shop. Chinaski said, Did I ever tell you that I used to
live above a porn shop? I shook ma head. He said, Well, I
did. It was cheap rent, fun too watching the men, the
lonely men, the young studs, the older women, the couples,
the curious and the underage, walk in and out of that
shop, sometimes fast, sometimes slow, sometimes giggling
and once a couple came out arguing, having it out right
there and then. The man socked the woman in the mouth.
There was blood everywhere. I was overlooking the crime
of the scene, wondering where I'd left ma boots, as I
wanted to go down and kicked that son of a bitch across
the road. Thinking was a waste of time. That woman with
the bust mouth, she went for him. She went for her man,
never seen anything so dirty. She dug her nails into his
hair, pulled his head down, so she could rip her nails into
his eyes. He was blinded. She took off her shoe and she
whupped him around the head, stuck a stiletto heel right
through the side of his jaw. He slumped to the floor, taking
the shoe with him and shouting blood. I forgot about ma
own shoes, went down to see what I could do, as much as
that guy deserved it I didn't want to see her kill him.
Rushing, I needn't have bothered, by the time I got down
the bottom of ma stairs and out on the street, she had his
head cradled in her lap, pulling the shoe out of his face,
murmuring softly, I'm sorry, baby. The man said nothing,
just put his fingers over the hole in his cheek, quiet in the
knowledge that in some ways he was loved.

We stopped walking. We were there. Chinaski and I looked
at the basket with yesterday's or the day afore's bread and
stuff in it. We looked up at the woman in the bake-house
looking at us, looking at the stale bread. She did a queer
thing then, she took a plastic bag, she put two old ice
buns, a rock-hard half of a French Stick and a small
brown. She put all that in the bag, gave it a twist, came

out the door and gave it to us. She said, That's for your dog. I just nodded, unable to find words supple enough to compound an unbelieved lie.

Assholes
In the World
Mine
And All

Those rare crazy moments, rare as a pound shop epiphany
and no sell by date, a time extended in space where I
wished for once that I was more sober. I must have looked
a mess, felt a mess, clothes crumpled as a crushed can of
beer, cheep beer. Chinaski came up behind, wondered why
I'd stopped in the doorway, why l hung around the
threshold of ma own door when it was cold outside and we
needed a piss. No wonder he was suffering, we'd held on
all the way back from a party, despite seeing plenty of
blind alleys and old fashioned phone-boxes. Chinaski
shoved me through the door, wanted to know what was
going on. There she was, ma sweet girl, in bed, a magazine
spread on the duvet cover and a small smoke in her hand.

Hi-ya, she said.

Ollreet, luv, din't expect you, like.

Want me to go?

Nah.

Good, clean your teeth and other bits that might come in
useful and get into bed!

I laughed, staggered through into the kitchen, closely
followed by Chinaski who somehow beat me to the loo. He
allus did that and I could never figure out how. He pissed
nosily, sang some sad song from the forties, while I made
do with the sink. I ran the geyser, stripped off and
clambered up and in ma sink -- times are when it pays to
be small. Couldn't believe it, but Chinaski was still

pissing, must have had a bladder of a horse. You'd think he'd finish, hear the drops tail off, then all of sudden, he was in nigh on full flow again. Between bouts of pissing, he had the nerve to say this to me, and it smarted, said, She's a bit common, your bit of cunt.

Good, I said, fuck the aristocracy.

Exactly.

Carry on pissing, ma friend, it's the only action your dick's getting this evening. Chinaski laughed at that and I squirted cheap washing up liquid under ma pits and around ma dick. Don't know if I over did that or the water around ma way was suddenly getting soft, seemed to be sat in that sink for years sopping the water off. Here, let me give you a hand, said Chinaski.

Fuck off, you snob, I said.

Hell, kid, meant nothing by it, said Chinaski, filling up a big pan that I used for spaghetti and sloshing it over me with shaking hands. I screamed, Chinaski had used pure cold and ma family allowance equipment were smaller than the nads you get on old Greek statues.

What you doing in there, said ma girl.

Blindfold DIY circumcision with a rusty blade, I said.

Don't be all night about it I want a shag.

I dried masel on a tea-towel because I couldn't afford anything bigger. Chinaski pulled on ma shoulder just as I set off for the bedroom. Chinaski said, Where do I get to sleep tonight. I shrugged, shrugged him off, couldn't think and couldn't care and anyway, I knew he'd stretch best he could, just like that time at the other party when he ended up sleeping in the bath. He'd be all right, I thought, even though we didn't have a bath.

I was cold and damp still and ma girlfriend was hot. We
spent hours, sucking and biting and frigging with each
other. First time, that room got warm since summer, we
were sweeting, kicking off the old mouldy duvet, kicking
off the bedspread, kicking the fuck out of the bedsprings
with at least three fucks that I could remember. They
weren't necessary, top rides each one, but they all felt
good. I had to go for a pee, came back and said to ma love,
You seen that. Ma prick looked like so much raw meat,
ragged and as unloved as a burst appendix. Give me that
here, she said. Ma sweet girl took me in, he kissed and
sucked and got it semi-up. Said that it's nay good, not up
to much, had too much to drink and not the stud I was.
She spat ma dick out then and laughed, laughed little
tears from her sweet brown eyes. She said, Since when
were you a stud? She had a point and I didn't answer. She
forced me back on the bed, her blond hair sure was a
mess, couldn't rightly see what she was up to, but it sure
was sore. I brushed her hair aside, found her sucking ma
spunk dry, found her draining me and playing with ma
ass. She popped a finger up and fucked me good. Mr
ragged little prick was tight and pumped up but still I
couldn't come. She finger-fucked ma ass and sucked and
nothing had ever been quite so close to pain afore, could
feel every scrape of her teeth, every flick of her tongue,
she took her mouth away to say, You will come in ma
mouth. Christ if only I could. I said, you sure, you want
this, not every one does -- most don't. I couldn't tell what
she said next, she was back on ma dick and I was feeling
comical, the way I couldn't come, the way she sucked with
two fingers up ma ass and Chinaski looking over her
shoulder, looking down approvingly and giving me the
thumbs up. Don't know what that woman hit, but ass,
prick and balls went into spasm and I was shooting more
muck than ever in ma life. Ma girlfriend caught most of it,
but she didn't catch it all, pulling her mouth off: spunk,
thin looking spunk, got sprayed around a bit. There
weren't, just weren't, any words at all handy around for

me to say how sweet-sweet it all was. I looked at ma
woman, spider-thread semen hung from her lips, two
fingers still crammed in ma arse, her lips, reaching out,
kissing me, tasting ma own cum, tasting ma own luck.
When we broke free she rubbed what little spunk was
around into her skin and we went and got cleaned up. We
shared a toothbrush, hers, we tried to get back into bed to
find, Chinaski there, fast on, drunk snoring, so we did the
best we could with a couple of coats and an old blue
dressing gown that had belonged to an uncle of mine.
Loved the whole world that night, even Chinaski shouting
in his sleep about the death of Mickey Mouse. Ma girl's
soft warm snores, snuggled into ma neck, ma tiny wizened
up prick and ma ass as raw as a bust heart.

Tomorrow, I promised masel'

I'd take on the whole world

go get masel' a job, tomorrow.

People

People allus try their best, try their bestest when they
come together. All that young, new, bright devouring love,
hungry as a grinning shark, brimming with good
intentions, and bad grammar. Old jokes come in useful,
you get into bed not with the one you love but all the
shags and half-shags you all had afore, and some of their
half shags and shags too, an infinite le grand tour of
shagdom. You try your best, you talk it through, the
putting it about you've been put through, you agree, afore
the condoms come off that the pair of yous will get
checked out. You have a shag, slip off the rubber things,
wring its wrinkly neck, `cos don't believe the adverts it is
not as good with as without. You wander down to the
special clinic wait in line, wait in waiting room on plastic
chairs by a table stacked with second hand magazines and
today is a mixed session and you don't make small talk in
a clap clinic. Chinaski was with me and not even we
talked, he read his Nietzsche and I read all the leaflets of
all the things out there you could get these days. I mun
have led a sheltered life, `cos I hadn't heard a dickie-bird
about two thirds of `em -- some real obscure stuff. There
were pictures, the world carved up according to clap,
major aid zones and all that. There was this wondrous
small picture of this Australian man who had picked up
something in, I think, Bali and half his knob had rotted
off. It was better than a horror show. I read this, like a
bairn, like a male bairn, scared and holding its dick. I
couldn't help it, embarrassing I grant you, nay bother,
especially in a mixed ward, but I read the name of what
he had in obsolete Latin and clutched the old goolies
hoping they wouldn't drop off -- not the biggest balls in
the world, smallest nads ma x had seen ever, but small or
not, I wanted them safely attached and working. I tried to
get a grip, mental and literal, of ma dick, Chinaski looked

up from some glasses he found in the bin, only one loop still on the frame, but he read good enough, I said, Chinaski have you seen this. He said, Man, I had that over thirty years ago, I enjoyed getting that, some heroin-head I was screwing, used to work the streets now and again to feed her habit and get takeways -- I liked those takeaways and I liked the dose she gave me more.

Chinaski, I said, you sure is a man of rare and exotic tastes. He agreed and said, One of the best ways of getting free health care over there is to go to a hospital with very social diseases. I went along with what that picture shewing and they gave me enough penicillin and tablets and shit to save half the third world. And, for reasons that I fail to understand, they even fixed ma teeth -- nothing fancy, but two bad teeth got taken out for free and I was pleased with the way they had dealt with me.

I looked at Chinaski in a whole new light. Strange ideas he had, but, the more you swilled them around your mind, the more likely you were due some brain damage. Having enough of the below the belt life, I found an old *Dalesman* magazine, read a poem about daffodils in Gunnerside by someone in Thirsk and I swore blind that if I ever had the money or a gun or some transport and some time to kill, I gan to Thirsk and whack the cunt that wrote about those daffodils. Feeling mean and evil and more than I little bored I helped masel' to some water, though Chinaski mentioned something about bromide and the lack of lead in your pencil. A young girl pushed past me as I was by the water, she took ma seat, no fucking shame. She didn't look old enough to do a paper-round and that's when I copped her. She was the girl that Mr Woodhall was banging. She was there with her friend, saying how the clap clinic was cleaner than the abortion ward. I wasn't about to turn Victorian about anything, but something seemed amiss. I stood by Chinaski, made a nod with ma head in the direction of the girls, said what they said. He shook his head and started going on about the thirties again, something about, how they fixed your shoes, car, how things were worth fixing back then. No idea what he was dribbling on about and they called ma name from a list, but not very well, as folk find it a difficult name to read or call out at all.

I did not enjoy having ma pipe pricked, the scrape, the samples they took and peeing a little blood. But I felt like I was doing the right thing. I felt that this was a rite, a rite of passage to fuck freely with a good, clean certified conscience. They said it would be at least two weeks afore I got the result. Chinaski moaned all the way out, said back in the thirties they could mend your shoes and car there and then and it stayed fixed.

I don't know, maybe back in the thirties they could do all that. But they couldn't fix syphilis, no way, Jose, no way, no fuck.

Fixed shoes seemed small comfort

even though we walked all the way

home and I limped still holding

ma screened and sampled dick.

By Terror Terrace
Just by Agony Way

Snuggling down late at night, it was throwing out time at
the Working Men's Club on the other side of the road,
there was a hint of frost in the air despite the wet
autumns of the last few years, ma sheets were moist with
the smell of ma woman, scrunched up like a ball, duvet
cover on top, sniffing from bottom, to cunt, to pits, to scent
of her hair on the pillow, drinking in her sour honey.
Chinaski had a cold, had a slug of whiskey and *Beecham's*
Lemonsip in a jam pot and he was swigging it back.
Shouting in the street, some woman crying. Shit, here we
go again, said Chinaski. He dragged the covers off and I
came to the small window that overlooked the terrace
street by. There was a man and he was ragging a woman
round. He was calling this woman: a bitch a whore a
fucking whore a fucking bitch fucking cunt of a fucking
cheating fucking bitch; he was ragging her around by the
hair and Chinaski said, put your pants on.

Chinaski had a cold, Chinaski was dead, a dead drunk old
man but he went out there to sort that man out. And me,
me in ma boxer shorts and t-shirt I went out there too. We
piled in on the man who was calling the woman all them
names without too good punctuation and nay sense of the
vocative case. We tried to stop that man hurting that
woman as he ragged her round by the hair and punched
her ribs in. We failed. Chinaski had a cold and was an old
man and dead already. I was young, had no excuse but
that thug was strong. He broke the woman's arm, badly,
bits of bone sticking up out of the reddening flesh, that's
how strong that man was and the police station just at the
top of the road didn't seem to care nor any of the passers
by, just me and Chinaski that man in the road with the
stamped on head, bust yellow teeth and broken nose

pissing blood and a small charva with tousled hair and none too clean boxer shorts and two sides of broken ribs and someone's fist constantly hitting the side of his head. Those two characters seem to care what was going on, the way that thug dragged the woman off home to slap her around some more, to call her all those names signifying hate, to go back to her home to terrorise the children, trash the place and beat a woman up some more -- that thug made plenty of pace, the woman dragged along behind like a comic scene from some kind of soap opera from the times of the Neanderthal, and Chinaski said to me through a bubbling gobbit of blood, he said to me, Me and you, buddy, were never cut out to be heroes. I tried to reply something straight away, but too winded and had a cry stuck in ma throat, eventually, I crawled over to Chinaski and said, Well, buddy, I ain't the one reading Nietzsche. Chinaski laughed at that and I laughed back. Despite it all, we laughed, we picked bits of each other up and we laughed all the way back to the gaff, hoping that it would kill the sound of that woman's cries and the thug, shouting, cunt fucking bitch fucking bastard cheating fucking cunting slit-arse bitch.

Dirty Old Man
Noted

In the centre of the fall of a long line of trees standing half
naked, half unstuck for leaves, Chinaski and I walked.
This lane went along the river. It went from town to our
digs. It was useful that way, till the floods came, making
us slip into a side-street, to find that we had gone past our
turn off anyway. Chinaski was pished about this, but I
could see no reason to care, back home nothing was in but
the rats and a diminishing pile of rice. They worked so
hard those rats, every day/every night, they climbed down
from upstairs to ma floor to add to their store, knowing
that we'd take at least a couple of panfuls out. They did
that and they carried on doing that and we carried on
with what we did and it was hard to suss who were the
biggest mugs, till you remembered whose rice it was in the
first place, thinking of Ralph Sing, the man above, falling
on hard times, living like us where no one should, not
even us.

We cut up by the river found a cheap butcher's, saw that
for a mere pound only we could buy a pack of bacon bits. I
was so happy. I said, Chinaski just think, only a pound
and we got ourselves a bacon butty with that stale bread
or chop bits up and put it to the rice and we got a bit of
fat, protein and variety, salty too, so save on that.
Chinaski shook his head, looked like he didn't really want
to tell me something, but knowing at the same time that
the thing would get told nonetheless. Chinaski said, We
don't have a pound.

What we got? I said, not believing our luck, the lack of
funds and the cheapest of bacon bits still beyond our
humble purse.

Eighty-seven pence is all, said Chinaski.

That settled it. We walked on, feeling weak, thinking how good that bacon would have been, thinking of the dull, bland taste of badly boiled rice, thinking about plain bread, burnt badly under the grill, thinking about having Lunch with the Archbishop of Canterbury at the Savoy as he spun the one liners about how blessed were the poor. Smug Proddy dawg.

We walked on.

We walked into an argument.

We stopped to gawp and look and laugh a little.

A tramp at the door of a church was giving a priest a hard time about the alms he receiving. I laughed at the happenstance, what with what I was thinking, that wag the Archbishop and his concern for a good port and the poor, and the fact, like a fat Dickensian coincidence, that I had the very same theological slight of hand on ma own doorstep...well, perhaps two streets down. Chinaski laughed for other reasons. He reckoned the fat priest had been ready to thump the tramp till we turned up. Chinaski was looking round for a bit of action, to see if anyone was up to set some odds on this. But there were just us and people busy walking on by on the other side of the street going blind in one eye.

Look, you've got fifty pence for a cup of tea and that's all, said the priest.

How can I get a drink for that, said the tramp.

There's St Margaret Clitheroe's charity tea rooms on the corner, said the priest.

No. A real drink. I'm an alcoholic. How can I get a drink for fifty pence, said the tramp.

A cup of tea would be better for you, said the priest.

80

Fuck that, I need a drink, said the tramp and Chinaski stuck his nose in and said, Better for you, you mean. Besides, you'd get your fifty pence back -- that Clitheroe place is one of your rackets.

Who asked you? said the priest, bustling in on Chinaski, which was a big mistake. The fat priest and the dead prophet slugged it out, round for round, pound for pound of flesh and the morality of fifty pence. The fat priest lashing out with a couple of the Credoes or a Hail Mary or two and Chinaski calling out that the man of God was a tight cunt who wouldn't give a sip of communion wine to a drowning man -- it was madness and the tramp turned to me and said, A drink for fifty pence that's just taking the piss. The tramp threw the coin on the floor and spat on it, though he missed, couldn't believe ma luck, thinking that tramps worked in mysterious ways as I picked up the coin, thinking of bringing home the bacon at last. The priest had had enough, after a while he stopped kicking Chinaski around and went inside to light a candle. Chinaski asked for a hand up.

Pretty Girl
With this House
for Rent

You don't understand, she said. I sure as hell didn't. We'd
just had some very satisfying sex, with her mate joining in
from time to time and a bottle of *Cava* and the very kinky
use of both big toes and now all of a sudden this woman,
this rather well to do woman with a house she was going
to rent so she could see the world, well she, this person in
question was biting ma shoulder, then shouting out you
don't understand. Perhaps, it was the new craze in parties.
I took masel' off the bed, the friend, still in the same bed,
was out for the count, her jag marks, bleeding a little, her
eyes saying a slow goodbye to reason, as the woman with
the house that she hoped to rent, was fingering her,
pinching her right pierced nipple, shouting, You don't
understand. I was awake and needing a pee and a talk
with Chinaski, I knew that much, happily I could do both.

Chinaski had crashed out in the bath, he'd gone up there
early unable to have a conversation with anyone that
mattered, unimpressed with the heroin thing a large part
of the party was getting into, and not getting into anyone's
knickers, Chinaski had taken himself somewhere to crash
while he got me back from the fuck session upstairs with
the woman who was in hopes of renting out her house.
The friend, the one who had joined in for some action had
come in from washing her cunt saying how there was a
dead drunk man asleep in the bath. Don't worry that's
only Chinaski, I said.

Well, he was asleep under a dripping cold tap and I pissed
in the sink and someone was using next door for selling
everything he had and whom I didn't like to disturb,
wasn't worth it, not just for a pipe full of piss. Chinaski, I
said, shaking the man and on the quiet side, as I didn't

want to really disturb him. Chinaski, I said again, a bit louder and shaking much more strongly.

Whatyouwan? said Chinaski.

You know that girl, you know the one I got it together with tonight, the friend too, all three in there making the beast with the multiple bad backs.

Don't bore me, said Chinaski, you should have made it up with that sweet girl from the coffee shop, so what if it was expensive and catered strictly for the upper class or tourist trade -- you know my feelings, you know the way I'm fixed about this.

Listen, Widehead, whose fault is it, I'm not seeing that girl.

Stop whining and what's happening? said Chinaski raising himself from between the taps, searching his pockets for something only semi-illegal to smoke.

Well, thought things were sweet, ganning off to sleep, not much room, three in the bed, when I wake up and she biting ma shoulder, saying that I don't understand.

Well?

I don't.

Well, you must admit that the lady has a point, get back in there; I'll wander in, take a look, maybe there is something I can do; what the hell, I've got a crick in ma neck.

I went back in, the woman I didn't understand was licking and frigging her sleeping friend, it looked like a cruel thing to do, but it filled out ma prick. As she was bent over tonguing, I bent down and had a lick of her, tasted ma own stale juice and the ghosts of farts. It got better. It would be pushing it to get much worse. Who knows. I still understood nothing, but popped ma prick in while ma mind got a hold on this. The lady with the house to rent, arched her ass up, looked on for it again and we savoured misunderstanding for a while.

I couldn't come. She didn't seem to mind, kept freeing a hand and sticking it up her friend or away with the nipples, hard dippled decorations with a slight halo of red hair around them. Truth was, I was getting a little bored. I would have withdrawn but since the night Chinaski fucked ma girl, I've felt less than a man, and I didn't think masel' much of a man to start with. So I ground on and on, till the woman who was hoping to have at least three months in India and two in Thailand said, I want a finish. I quickened up, filled ma mind with sick, horny thoughts, but no good. Chinaski rolled up, pulled up a chair by the bed, by me, then started slapping ma ass as I drove ma dick in. Chinaski must have one hell of a sense of timing, sense of rhythm, `cos I've got none at all. The woman with the house was laughing, she was thrusting her hips, bum and cunt back at me and Chinaski was banging ma ass and prick back inside her. He slapped, she laughed, he slapped and she laughed, then a couple in the next room who said they had to fly from Manchester early next morning, asked us to can it a little. We told `em to fuck off. I said, Fuck off, fuck off, fuck off, fuck off. Chinaski slapped, the woman laughed and finally I came, just a thin trickle, just a wee buzz, but the relief -- well, should have heard that woman laugh. The folks next door did, they packed up and left there and then -- lucky old Manchester.

Chinaski, eased back into his seat, re-lit the doff that had gone out, said, You still nothing but a stupid fuck monkey, go see that girl, man she's sweet.

You'd know, I said.

I do, now go.

84

Dictation from a Dirty Old Man

I woke up, it was dark I was in ma room, we had made it back, but I didn't know how, didn't know the names of the week and who they were friendly with: Was Tuesday best marras with Thursday still, and what was that tiff atween Monday and Sunday all about -- who cares who is the first day of the week. But all that was minor, `cos everything jumping about, rushing together, breaking up and falling apart. I had it bad, but not like Chinaski had it. He had his with a passion and a serving to go of fries on the side.

Woke up, there's Chinaski at the window and he is crying. Through his trickle of tears he says out loud on that small world of stage we renting, he saying this, broken and low and only just audible: What they done to the sun? What they do that for? Man, we are screwed, how could we let we do that to we? That poor sun, that poor sky, man, even the stars they come out to weep at this, at what we done at last.

I said, Chinaski, come back to bed, that's the moon you looking at. This is two am in the morning and day don't start round here at this time of year for at least six hours -- me tell you for true, get back in the bed, wipe them tears and stop reading Nietzsche: that Polish pretending sick prick ain't doing you no good. The *Gay Science*? The *Joyful Wisdom*? You didn't laugh once and you still wouldn't demand your money back.

You're a fine one to talk, said Chinaski, turning round framed by a bastard halo of light spun from a full moon. He said, You make me laugh, you still learning nothing, venturing nothing, you like what that Dane said...Chinaski didn't continue, he just shook his mane of moonlight, turned back to the window, and apologised one more time for all that we had done to the sun. I scratched ma memories for a while, came up with something I still felt blue about. It got me shouting at Chinaski again, all we seemed to be doing these days was arguing, but he had no right to bring up the Dane.

You leave her out of it. I liked her, could have loved her, wanted to see her more, she was canny, just lost her address, couldn't remember the name of the hotel, know it was in Crief or something like that, wanted to see her again, wanted to make love to that long, slender beautiful girl, but I lost the address and I moved out...Hope I didn't hurt her, hope some day we'll meet again, if only to say sorry. She was canny, ma fault, lost the address, you got no right at all bringing her up, you wasn't even there!

Chinaski turned from bothering the moon with his woe for the sun. He turned around to me, put his finger to his lips, tried to quieten me down. I was in no mood for that, just after losing another love. Who would be. He said, There you go again, lost in the past, can't move forward, can only stare back. That's what I mean, didn't mean to bring up Ulla, but bang like a mental missile you went straight back to that crippled past -- just one of the too frigging many guilty pasts you gotten. Well, buddy, what I wanted to talk about was what Søren Kierkegaard once said, something about, you have to live life forward, but understand it back. That's what I was getting at. But you, you just break your balls with the past, understanding nothing, so much so, can't even live it forward no more.

Got out of ma sick bed, felt rajed, went up to Chinaski to smack him in the head and I saw what we had done to the sun, felt too lousy to argue.

Days like Three
Legged Donkeys

You know, they'll say you are mad, dismiss everything you say or write or think, `cos you mad. Doesn't matter if you are mad or not, they'll say you are mad, then you can be dismissed. You know what I'm saying here, you understand the full implications of you letting me doss down here, what people will think -

All right, Chinaski, change the record man, I said.

They'll dismiss --

How maddening, I said.

Can't talk sense to you this morning.

`Course not, I'm mad, I said.

You're fucking irritating -- what's gotten into you?

Re-reading *Three Men in a Boat*.

Why?

It reminds me of the Czech Republic.

How?

Well, long story, but that book was one of the most readily available foreign books to be had afore they threw out the ghost of Joe Stalin and broke the country in half and started beating up Gypsies in the name of democracy.

Can the soap-box, back with the boat. So!

Well, it was available, the Czechs they read it, they liked it, and they even thought that the English sense of humour was the same as the Czech sense of humour. So, I re-read Three Men in a Boat and I get reminded of the Czech Republic.

Yep, but what I want to know is why you do this to yourself -- why you wanting to remind yourself with memories of the Czech Republic.

What is this, *In the Psychiatrist's Chair* with that smug Mick and his piss-poor platitudes. You ain't Sigmund Freud, you ain't strung out on Jungian theory -- Christ one of the things I dig about you is that you never fell for that crap. So, don't you dare come the comfy couch with me and ask me did I want to kill ma Mam and Dad. Course, I did, who wouldn't?

Don't side-track yourself, and don't bullshit me. You reading this, `cos you thinking about that young Czech girl. I saw you getting out those old photos the other day. Man, she left you with a lump of ice in your heart, fucked you around, messed up your head, leaving you humping your memories and re-reading books not worth reading in the first place.

What's it to you? I'm enjoying this...it's bullshit. I ken that. I think about when it was written, the class of people it represents, the class of reader it attracted and I think back on the hard times back then for the people not laughing, not reading; aye, I think those things, and I laugh, laugh for revenge, that me, Mr No Money, Mr No Prospects, Mr No Ambition with no where to go, that's me that is reading this and having the last laugh.

You bullshitting me again. You reading this `cos you want the memories back of the Czech girl: that's all and that's that.

Well, so what, many the good wank I've had thinking about that lass.

Me too, said Chinaski and we both had the last laugh.

Fire Station

Chinaski, Chinaski, I shouted, sweating joy, a fifty pence piece tightly held atween ma fingers, so tight, could have been denting the nickel on the side. Chinaski was still pished, dusting himself down, promising to call back later and burn the fat priest's kirk down. I said, Kirk is one of ma words -- old Yorkshire -- you don't say kirk.

Chinaski said, Kirke, happy now? What is it with you and language, leave it alone. What you whining about now?

The tramp was still there muttering about fifty pence and its lack of efficacy as far as a token of charity goes. The tramp muttered, Chinaski, dabbed at the scratch marks in his face and I held on to the fat priest's fifty pence like it was Willy Wonka's golden ticket. Chinaski, I said, I've got the fifty pence, fifty pence added to eighty-seven pence is ... well, it's enough to get that pack of bacon bits-

Bacon bits! Chinaski roared, you want to talk about bacon bits at a time like this. This man here needs a drink. What is it with you, what is it you fail to understand?

...?.. I don't know, hadn't an answer, never seen Chinaski so mad, not even when he found out he'd been wiping his ass with imaginary toilet paper -- boy, he was real pished and the tramp stomped around muttering for a drink, cursing the fifty pence piece and fat priests, muttering and moving just like a deranged dancing bear without a grant from an arts council for the playing of the hurdy-gurdy.

I've got an idea, it was the drunk, he hadn't a razor, a bar of soap, but he had an idea. I knew how he felt. He said, there is a row of shops in a certain part of town, two of the shops are boarded up, but one, a general store, has everything including a licence to sell wines and spirits. So far, this didn't sound like much of an idea. I knew the part of that town, knew nearer places where they had the same licence and a better range of beverages. Worse, who cares what the range is when we only had a pound odd of change and I still wanted those bacon bits. Chinaski though was listening as the drunk went on to talk about the garages round the back, the extension round the back of the shop, that there was a weak skylight. That it was possible to clamber on up, break in, drop down, help yourself to some gear and get out: with three of us on the job, it wouldn't take long.

It sounded like an old chocolate advert: all because the tramp's an alcoholic. Sun, smeared, weak yellow hung low in the sky, as Chinaski and the tramp walked in front to a wrong end of town, while behind, for luck, fifty pence was still tightly held, ma head in bits: bacon, hash-browns, eggs over-easy and beans on the side.

Post Office

Burning sorrow, tight in ma gut, some Japanese sword, twitching for a ritual, content with the smile of its edge to spill your guts, your bleeding life and all the pointless hours you've spent trying to save some reason for tomorrow's breath. The dole cheque had come. It had been cashed. Chinaski and ma girl and me were pissed. We had, I think something like fifty-two pounds to last the fortnight. We had I think, little left, just binging it down, talking red-face and mad in love with everyone, including our selves or souls or whatever metaphysical take on the after life we were taking with our beers, our shorts on the side, and tabs smoked down to the cardboard acrid with ash. We had all that, talked out of death life experiences, our weirdest trips, our most shameful thing done when drunk. Made `em cry with some of ma tales, made `em laugh with some others and couldn't think if their responses were appropriate or not, or if it mattered or, if so, mattered to whom...too many conjunctions, if and buts...getting in the way of an approaching full stop to really hang a frame on what was being said, heard or ignored in the raising of glasses and spliff smoke. Said I was sorry, said I was sorry to a dear friend, that it was just the jerk of ma words that came out, then the embarrassed laugh at what I said, not the contents, then ma head exploding, talking shit, rotten with words, necrosis rabid in the rapid speech of this disintegrating mind that I had, and I'm so sorry, Anna, sorry bad...

Apparently, ma lips were still twitching, but nothing was coming out. Chinaski helped himself to some money in ma pockets, bought the drinks, got in the round -- good man, Chinaski, good man. This was our one day/night/morning out a fortnight and so far no one had thrown us out. But ma mind, kept stuttering remorse and shame. It got boring, Chinaski and ma girl, that sweet swirl of gold, kissing me goodbye, saying that they would be back later to pick me up from the floor and drag me home. Hoping they wouldn't be long, ma mind having another go at me, filching every hurt thing up, wounded as a pinned butterfly; said sorry for what I'd done, for what I hadn't done, even for what they said I'd done and hadn't; had a go at feeling guilty for that, for a change, never done it afore, had me hollering, had me shouting out; they had me thrown out, banging ma head on tables and chairs, as they shoved me out the door into the cold, the relentless rain and that ache of solitude you feel hearing others laugh and talk and crack, tucking into life like a hearty meal with no bill in sight.

Don't know how I got home. I know Mrs Woodhall let me in and she looked worried, but her problems weren't ma problems and no I hadn't seen her bum of her husband and no, I didn't really care if their son had run out, looking for him with a shotgun. I couldn't care `cos I thought I'd done with caring that night, till I opened ma door, found Chinaski, ball deep in ma woman, fucking her hard and she enjoying, seeming to enjoy it, so much more, what that dead drunk man was putting down.

Night, Mrs Woodhall.

Go `long in, and you take care, son.

Mockingbird Come Back
Come Mock Me
Some More

Days afore I took ma tongue, voice-box and mental
equipment and shook some talk atween the gaps and
spaces atween Chinaski and me. Could have spent the
rest of our lives like Trappist monks on the piss and on
the quiet. Could have let Chinaski walk out ma door and
not said a word of farewell. Could have let Chinaski put a
bullet in his head, watch his body kick and not say a word.
Sometimes you feel so smug and important with yoursel,'
kidding everyone that you are right there in the spaces
that the young Wittgenstein talked about, where words
don't help, can't have meaning and the mystic keeps his
gob shut. You keep your lips together, keeping stum,
saying nothing and smug with second hand Gnosis.

You are not Wittgenstein

You are simply

sulking.

The silence didn't last. Chinaski said, Will you just take a
look at that. It was the rats and they were struggling.
Moving out as a pack, up the walls, back up the wall, up
the hole and back into Ralph Singh's place, carrying as
best they could what was left of their rice. Would you just
take a look at that, said Chinaski.

All right, I heard already.

Ain't it something?

Suppose.

Man, I can't bear to see them struggle, Chinaski stood at the foot of the wall, near the rotten skirting boards, hunkered down and made himself a human ladder. Rats, they crawled up him and over him and scampered up the walls. I didn't want to see them go, neither did Chinaski. For spite I said, See, we should have bought those bacon bits after all. He collapsed, Chinaski lay on the floor and wept, punching the floorboards, fighting for his breath as the laughter came, bubbling up, volcano roar, hot with mirth and madness, hot wave of laughter broke over me, bathed, baptised me in derision and shrove ma soul of the sickness of seriousness. We lay down and laughed against the far wall, watching rats fight gravity, using our bodies as ladders, laughing and glad too for a hand up out of there.

Sometime after the last laugh was spat, I said to Chinaski about the party we'd gotten invited to later that night -- old friends, some woman's going away party. Chinaski said it was time that he said goodbye too, but not tonight.

I was glad. Of all things, I took out ma clarinet and played an old quiet, blues. Chinaski said, If you play any more I might just change ma mind. He punched me in the arm and had another laugh.

There are times

when nobody knows

how laughs

are hurting.

Erectulations
Madhibitions
Ordinary Tales
of Generality

Like a man in a storm waiting for the last bus home, I
waited for ma happy times to show up, wanking masel'
silly for the want of the love, for the want of somebody to
fuck, for the wantonness in ma head, that saw good sex
everywhere `cept inside the four walls of ma room; I
waited for K, I waited three times for J, waited too long for
V, waited till I almost caught the bus over when she said
don't come (sorry that was M.) Realised, what sad
bragging I had, could have used a lot of the letters of the
alphabet, some of `em more than once and even strange
ones like X, Z and Q. It wasn't the letters that mattered,
nor, even at the end, what they signified. It was been
dyslexic with lack of love and the dull thud of pulling your
prick, spitting out all the maps of the world where you
ain't never been, never going, do not pass go, do not collect
two hundred pound, move directly to gaol, get bum-fucked
by the ward hubba, get aids off a dirty needle, have your
brains eaten while still conscious by the prison psycho -
not allus an inmate.

Bad way, bad way and no mistake, kept shouting out
letters of the alphabet, but Chinaski was there to trot to
the shops for some kind of booze, whiskey or whisky or
cider or stout or cooking rum, once, that wasn't too bad if
you were hard-smashed first. Chinaski looked after us, but
said this had got to stop. I agreed, finally, throwing up into
his lap, wiping ma mouth on his old denim jacket, the one
he could fill at one time with muscle and spite. Harder
man than me, Chinaski, allus was, allus will be a harder
man than me. I was weak. I couldn't even turn a page of
Nietzsche and Chinaski read it like the Dandy or a

telephone directory.

Felt like a hippy fraud, all this talk of love and all I really wanted to do perhaps was ease ma prick into something soft and happy for it. If you like love so damn much, how come every time you had it, had it good, you threw it away? That's what Chinaski said and I had no answer. Thought F.

Anything left to drink? I said.

Sure, sure there is. There probably allus will be, for a while yet. But don't die a little each day, do it all at once, take a drink of the dark and knock it back in a oner. Don't get to be an old ugly drunk. Don't get so that you can curse a man in good conscience for only giving you fifty pence.

Knew Chinaski was right that's why I sent him out on a mission to collect from various chemists, pharmacies and drugstores all that headache gear. Sent him out too for two bottles of cava: two for six pounds, special offer from Asda. I was happy.

It took two hours, seventeen minutes and three to five seconds to open all the tablets. We can't be more accurate than that as our eyes were bleared.

By that time that cava was nicely chilled. We knocked it back, slug for slug, each mouthful I took I drank in a cocktail of tabs to kill the pain that should have been in ma head. I remember reaching the end of the bottle and still plenty left, remember Chinaski finding some still strong cider, just one can, left by oversight from last night. I remember as I drank all them tablets down that I was mortal `cos that can tasted just as good as the fine cava that we'd been drinking.

Chinaski was there for me. As I puked ma stomach out.

He'd catch it with glasses, with bowls with anything and make me drink it back up. Don't know how many times I drank ma own vomit, thick with half-mashed tablets, thick with bits of blood. I drank and I puked and I drank some more, but allus puked more than I drank and Chinaski knew what he was doing. For when I finally woke the next day, I couldn't stomach death no more. I looked at the room, I looked at the way I was living and it was strong enough to kick me out of bed and start getting along again with pain; every cripple having their own way of waking.

This weak voice said, this voice of mine, aching for good clean water, this voice say, What next?

Chinaski walked into the kitchen, came back with a bundle of black bin liners. He said, Time we paid that washeretta another God damn visit.

Ma life a cycle

at a cheap launderette

No. 5 @ 40 degrees

with a strong rinse

and spin.

No North
of No North
And South
Don't Matter

Never have this time again, all I was doing was feeling
sorry for it, the way that piece of time couldn't come back,
though feeling pretty glad that at least this part moment
was over. Never get the minute back and all I could think
to do was note it down, briefly on the back of ma summons
notice, that this time wasn't going to get another chance.
It was over, redundant, and someone came knocking at ma
door with a baseball bat and a photograph that did not
look unlike me.

Is this you? the man said.

What do you think? I said.

I think there is a certain likeness.

Well, in that case, he could be ma brother.

Is he in?

He in't.

Will he be back?

Nay, he never lived here in the first place.

You sure this isn't you?

Are you?

No.

Well, that's two of us, in this world that is something for
sure.

I don't like hitting the wrong guy?

Who would?

A psycho, I suppose.

Suppose you're right.

Well, if you see your brother, tell him that I'm looking for him.

And you are?

I'm the man with the baseball bat.

Right you are then.

I watched the man with the baseball bat walk down the path, to his waiting black car and I felt sorry for him. It was one of those days that I felt sorry for everyone in some way or one way or another. Just the way it goes. Got so glad knowing that this part of time was washed up and finished like bottles left out for the milkman in the rain -- just like that -- though knowing, that this mood would sometime soon come round again, regular as clockwork.

The gate swung open, Chinaski walked down the path, bottles clinking, said, Hey Chinaski, you better watch out, you look a bit like ma brother. You was almost in time for a hiding.

Chinaski said, Don't bother me, man. I'm not ma brother's time keeper. We left it like that, somewhat confused around the syntax, while I searched for a corkscrew, finding that ma watch had stopped.

Burnt Water
Drowns Flame

You don't mind me being on, my girl said. I didn't. What I minded was Chinaski talking away to the shadows in the corner about this that and having a bit of the other. My girl's cunt was right over me, sitting on ma face, spilling juice and joy down ma throat. Strange thing, her clit seemed not only to swell but to grow long, plenty to play with, plenty to tongue. Poor girl ganning crazy, gripping the back of ma head hard, digging her nails in, rode ma head, like she was some kind of stud out to headfuck me. I loved it, loved her loving it more.

Chinaski said, You know some men don't give women the old tongue routine, says that it makes them effeminate, that they really faggots wanting to blow men -- you know that?

World full of strange notions, Chinaski, such like God's favourite pensioner is the Pope or Queen Bess the Second of England.

Exactly, who gives a damn about that. I'm bothered about all those men and their women friends missing out on some pretty good action.

How bothered are you?

Bothered enough to mention it. Now don't you mind me, get back to it, you doing fine.

Ma sweet girl was rubbing herself slow against ma lips. She pressed a bit more and I stuck in ma tongue. She quivered, slipped a fart out, apologised and carried on with riding ma head. She went round the course one more time, shaking ma tongue up her cunt, against the bump of her clit, felt her nails dig deep, felt back ache coming on,

felt glad about it all, watching her body dance all over ma
face, the way her boobs, fell and rocked against her body;
the way when she came again she squeezed her tits hard
and muttered someone else's name. Don't know who he
was, but he must have been good, the way she shuddered
to a stop and moaned.

You think they'd teach decent sex education these days,
Victoria's day is long gone, said Chinaski, helping himself
to the remains of ma bottle of *Paddy's* whiskey.

You think they'd teach indecent sex education and have
done with it, I said and Chinaski laughed, poured ma
sweet girl and me a glass. I asked ma girl if I could kiss
her some more. She said, she'd had enough. Is there
anything I could do for you, she said. I said, help yourself.
She said, I noticed that clean washing you brought back
hasn't been ironed yet. She said that and laughed, then
sucked me off. I could barely cum for laughing -- ma sweet
girl, ma sweet-sweet woman -- she was mad, thank God.

Chinaski was in a brown study

with a bottle of Paddy's

while ma girl and me

brushed our teeth

sharing the same toothbrush,

as Chinaski bad-mouthed

the whole damn world

from the depths of his study.

Fac to Tum

Stumbling cold outside, a sliver of bone moon, hanging in
the sky, some small rain clouds drifting by and Chinaski
cold already, what with sleeping in the bath. Shrammed to
the core, he struggled along, moaning about the shit awful
country he'd ended up spending death in. He moaned it
like a Blues, moaned it slow, least half ways home.

So, Chinaski, you didn't rate the party?

Saw enough of that shit the first time round. What did I
want to see fuckwits getting wasted on horse, snorting,
spiking, double-flush and daring each other into ma world
with unseeming haste. The women, that posh woman's
women friends all hated me, hated everything I had, even
the honesty, how can you hate honesty. What do they
know...think they know it all. They think they can judge
you too, act smug and self-righteous with it. It's like
history, like reading history, if all you do it for is just to
beat someone up with guilt then forget it. You German
bastards, you Roman bastards, you British bastards, you
English bastards, you northern bastards...fucking Catholic
bastards...

We were by the kirk of the fat priest and Chinaski wanted
to go in and fight some more. I wanted a sit down, too
much drink, too much smoke, too much boning and too
little food had me knee trembling all the way in and down
to a pew. Chinaski laughed, lewd and hard, up there in
front of a white looking Christ on his cross, up there
shaking his dead fists, shouting, Hope they're good quality
nails -- you hanging for a long, long time yet, buddy.

It was dark, that smell that only unloved places had, cold
and damp and taint of mice, poor as they are. Hanging on
to the seat in front, down on ma knees, knowing no longer

any prayer or praise that could matter, knotted with hunger and head pain. Chinaski strolled down the central aisle, as if looking for someone, someone important with whom he just might like to start a fight. Instead, he found me.

So, that fuck good, at the party, where you left your pal in the bath to get cold and shaky while you drank the cunts of two sweet things and got your nuts off. You liked that! You think it makes you doncha?

There was darkness, only the very white Christ showed, looking nothing like an oppressed Palestinian just about to set off and hound hell. He looked more like the dude on a friend's life-study class who talked about nearly meeting someone from Led Zeppelin -- can't quite remember what he said -- it impressed no one. Chinaski was by ma side, praying for a fuck soon, for a suck, for some taste of pussy or a drink or perhaps something to eat, babbling his prayers out to the empty pew in front.

You know I've done nothing for so long, I said. Chinaski shook his head. Once, I could never ends things, allus had three to four projects on the go...just lately, can't start, can't even start...nothing to get started about.

Give me a Jewish virgin to fuck, eyes like bust black grapes, moustache like Hitler who doesn't mind spawning a bastard to fuck the whole world with.

Shut it, Chinaski. This ain't funny...besides, I'm trying to say something here. Monk-

Let's play Monk and Nuns then.

Monk, genius, his music, his mind, the way it weaves in the brain, that complexity, you discover these people and genius don't cover what they really are...Parker dead when thirty four and all that music, all that change he brought about...Mingus-

What is this? Kissing ass of the great Jazz dead weak --
which cock-sucking saint we pray to for that?

Shut it, Chinaski, you leave the Jazzmen out of this. I'm
just saying got nothing left to give.

You sure gave those rich bitches in that party plenty --
maybe you should go in for porn?

Leave it.

Ain't leaving nothing...why don't you give that sweet girl
of yours a ring?

Why, so you can shag her some more?

Chinaski walked off and left me to spit in the dark, all the
hateful thoughts I ever had to give anyone, anything or
any god. Chinaski left me with the dark for a while, while
he went to see if he could find where the priest hid the
drink and grub.

Tell you what we do, said Chinaski, back from checking
the floor for dropped coins. Tell you what. Why don't we go
over there, grab that bitch in blue from the candle stand
and fuck her.

The Virgin Mary.

That's the bitch, we go over there, we lift up her skirts and
we give her what she ain't never had. Man imagine that,
you suffer labour pains and you ain't even had the fun
side of the deal -- like she some Friesian heifer or
something and it's artificial insemination week.

You sick.

We go over, two of us, a back and front manoeuvre, you up

104

the front, I'll do her ass.

You sicker than sick.

Imagine that, we have us our own little orgy down here.

Stop that.

Don't worry, nothing to fear. Her son looks kind of tied up.
He ain't gonna save no one.

Leave this now.

You fucking little bog-trotter. You play at everything, that's
why you dry. Take your skin off, your poxy English
liberalism and underneath, you just a frightened little
bogman with his breviary, rosary and forelock tucked up
your ass. You ain't gonna fuck the Virgin Mary, you ain't
gonna drive a stake through Jesu's heart, you ain't fit
enough for something new, too busy sucking on the Pope's
ring, and so deeply thankful, amen.

Chinaski ran out of words,

Christ still on his cross

while, for the moment, at least,

his mother's knickers were still

on, leaving me without a prayer

for anything other but a decent hell.

Love is a Dog from Hell

You talk yourself into a corner and forget that you drew
the map, you jaywalk the road you decide to travel by and
when you raise the stop sign in front of your own eyes,
`cos of highway repairs, you still jump forward, cheat and
give the finger to the fool bearing down on you from the
opposite side...You talk an extended metaphor, just to take
your mind away from Chinaski on the roof of this shop in
the wrong part of town. You think of a hundred and one
diversions, all washed out similes, tricks of the trade for
morons who don't really want to write -- just imitate well.
You've got your bag of tricks out, deciding what point of
view you gonna stage this scene and the protagonist, don't
give a fuck. He's up of the roof, banging his fist against
some perspex, trying to break his way in to somewhere
where some liquor's stored. Chinaski is failing. The drunk,
hollers, orders me to give a hand. I give him the finger
with one hand and only one hand, `cos I'm still holding the
fat priest's fifty pence in the other and I'm wishing to hell
that this sorry part is soon over as I want to buy some
bacon bits.

Good job, Rebekah threw you over, said Chinaski, shouting
down from the roof. Her family were right to piss you off.
You turn Jew for that girl's hand, when you can't stand
the thought of not having a sniff of bacon -- schmuck!

Chinaski allus knows how to hurt. There was some pain
coming, as I fought off the past, given up on that, mind on
the present, the job in hand, as I still clung on to that fifty
pence, that I weren't giving up. Not for nobody. Not for a
nobody like Chinaski.

Find me a brick, said Chinaski, a brick, something heavy
and I'll soon bust in and get us something to drink -- man,
I'm real dry now, need a drink as bad as that drunk.

Go up and give him a hand, said the drunk.

There this neighbourhood that I don't like, there is a bag
of bacon bits that I wish to buy, some drunk orders me to
give a hand to a madman on the roof, wonder what it feels
like to be the hand of god with the puppet-glove off.
Walking over to the wall, to the drainpipe that Chinaski
had shimmied up, quicker than a shit-house rat, and a
gang of Asians walk our way, walk down gobbing on the
ginnel's floor, shouting out that this is a Paki zone, that it
is time for us to leave, if we want to leave in one piece.
Chinaski, I shout up, it's time to come down. We ain't
welcome round here.

Chinaski says, tell `em to fuck off back to Pakistan if they
don't like it here; if they've got something against whites;
tell the shit-brown mother-fuckers that I did the job no
white man did, that I was young and strong and-

You're not young and strong now, Grandad, call me a shit-
brown motherfucker again and I'll fucking knife you.

Chinaski could never take a hint, he says, Why don't you
tell `em how you fancy the tits off their sisters, that you
dig North Indian or Paki women, why don't you tell `em
that and that you make a mean curry?

That was funny, Chinaski up on the roof, giving it out, a
drunk in the phone-box ordering a fire engine so he could
get up on a roof and lend a hand to a man robbing some
store for some liquor; funny, not seeing the one that hit,
funny that after a while, as they all laid in, I couldn't feel
a thing; sad, that this is the time that racism starts to eat
into your bones; sad, but not surprising.

Women

It was three in the morning, `cos I looked, checking the watch that ma father had given me when last we had met, nothing much to say, although I got to dig his garden over. When I said ma goodbye, t'ald man put his second best watch in ma hand, explained how that watch was for me, that if I would only take good care of it, it would keep good time, but if I fucked about, left it places, took it swimming or jumped in the bath or gan round rough-housing ma ass through life, then that watch would be sure to suffer. I looked at that watch, then at ma father, then I thanked him. Guess I hurt that man enough without saying anything against the watch he'd given me for turning a spade in a few yards of shale-thick soil. Never told him that the first thing I did was to get it fixed on the market cheap, four pounds and fifty three pence. It was four pounds that I didn't have, but, at least, I had something from ma father apart from unastounding looks.

Well, that watch, I looked at it full in the face; must have been keeping reasonably clean, but five minutes out of kilter with what that nice woman told me, repeatedly, on the telephone service provided by a mobile phone that Chinaski had picked up somewhere, sometime recent. Not that I asked him just where the hell had he been, how had he come back with two bottles of tequila, a teenth of Taliban Red and a mobile phone...I had questions, I would have wished for answers, but it was too much like effort at three in the morning to stumble him with all the questions I had lined up, both big and small and under-important. Besides, it wasn't the mystery of Chinaski that had me up with all the lights in ma gaff on, when I should have been sleep searching. Nay, had a tune in ma head for the first time in eighteen months. Felt like weeping for shame or joy or pure inadequacy.

Shamed me. I took ma clarinet out and it shamed me. I spent an hour, soft blowing some life into it and getting nothing you'd want to call tuneful. Breves -- remember them? I played scales in breves: harmonic, melodic, throughout all the range of that old second world war clarinet. Funny, it was only after I'd done ma scales that I realised that the instrument was something else given to me by ma father. Chinaski, didn't bat an eyelid. We shared tequila; I took a draw off his joint now and then, especially as he tried to ring somebody stateside on this strangely found mobile phone. It sure was mobile, `cos at four in the morning, still having no joy, he threw that phone through the window. It was quite a good shot, considering the state we were in and the small windows with which those bedsits were framed.

Chinaski was bitter. Chinaski paced around the threadbare carpet of ma room and I played. First time in a long time that I played. Chinaski didn't like it, but I played nonetheless. What you playing that Yiddish shit for! said Chinaski.

Wrong. It's Rom shit, I said.

What?

Roma, Kallomanush, Zincalli, Shinte, Hadooks, Zott, Vlak...I would have said more by the way of a reply, but I said it with ma clarinet. I played, ``A Tzigan went to Town to buy a Ghoraidh, brought home a Monisha''. I played that old tune, played it through the heavy, crass-heavy sentimental tears that spilled into the morning, played it through all the colours of emotions bubbling up through ma body and breathed, breathed out like a death-rattle, into that old clarinet of ma fathers; an instrument older than me, seen the second world war afore they cracked me open upon the world -- played it all.

There came a banging on the walls. I carried on playing.

There came a knocking on ma door. I carried on playing.
There came Mrs Woodhall walking into ma room, with her
dressing gown shewing her beautiful legs and her face
shewing her husband's handiwork. I stopped playing. But
not crying.

Delightful and wholesome as unexpected is the comfort of
strangers. I mean, I didn't even know Mrs Woodhall's
name. She said, Son, Lad, tha can't play like that at four
in the bloody morning. She said this matter of fact, nay
malice, she said this holding ma head to her falling
breasts, long, low loping breasts, already losing out to
gravity but still glorious to me. I held one. Ma left hand,
just dipped in and took her breast. She laughed, pushed
ma hand away, said, Stop that. So I did, but still couldn't
work out what her hubby was doing chasing bits of kids
when he had his beautiful wife, this woman even, to be
with, to cherish, to hold, to suck, to finger, to poke, to fuck,
to love...maybe, even love might be possible. Why not? I
loved her already, her bust nose and lips, the old bruised
black blood, hanging like a used tea-bag from her eye.
Pitiful. Pain cold as Kansas blues lying in your stomach
seeing that beautiful face all mashed up. She said, Lad,
Lad, what you gonna do? Tha can't carry on like this:
landlord after thee for one, then them fines and all the
rest. But more than that, Lad, tha can't go on like this.
She said this to me, a woman, a walking punch-bag,
holding ma head against tits, dog-eared as a lay-preacher's
bible. I said summart then, can't remember what, I think I
telt her that I loved her, that her husband was a fool, was
an arsehole, that I was gonna kill him just as soon as I
grew up or sobered up or her son came back with the gun.

She ragged me round. She said, stop that. She stood over
me. Her dressing gown fell apart just like a cheap porn
movie. She was beautiful. I couldn't care that her bikini
line was the biggest pair of mohair knickers that I'd ever
seen, nor that there was white and grey bedding down
with the curly brown. I didn't care, still said what I

wanted to do if she wanted to do. Looked up, first time noticed tears in her own eyes too. She took ma hand, spread out the fingers and frigged ma hand against her cunt and clit for awhile. She kissed ma fingers, kissed the brow of ma head goodnight.

Night, Mrs Woodhall.

Goodhall is ma husband's name, said Mrs Woodhall. Why don't you call me Marie.

Okay, Mrs Woodhall, night now and you take care.

Night...night, Son, and God bless.

She shut the door and Chinaski said, ironic like, said, God Bless -- that mother-fucking fraud. I didn't care. I got out the music papers and I wrote a score. it was all that I had been leading up to. It was that tune in ma head. I got it all, dotted it down, as Chinaski drank himself into sleep and snored. I was happy. I got the papers, neatly shuffled, I got `em with ma rest and I packed ma clarinet away, saw ma beat up, soprano sax, felt the urge strong to try playing the tune there and then, felt that music like the blood beat in ma ears, heart and head. But I saved it, this tune was too important to waste. Too tired for a tune like that to do it justice.

Checking the watch it said, six thirty seven. I turned off the light. Then I heard it. Out of the sleep-crippled dark came the sound of next door. Mr Woodhall getting up, giving Mrs Woodhall hell, it was loud, woke Chinaski. Good job. Chinaski stopped me going out with a carving knife in ma hand and dirty boxer shorts. He said, Don't kill a man dressed like that. What would your mother say or a bus driver for that matter.

Men, men such bastards, I said.

He said, Don't give me that...that's just `nother cheap way
of slapping their ass. They just as bad: all of us, just as
bad as bad gets...Don't mistreat 'em with bland nice --
don't bullshit. We're all just the same, the same ways we
all different.

Chinaski said that while they really kicked off in there. I
took out ma soprano sax. I played ma new tune. I played it
with all ma heart, with all ma love, played like I never
wanted to play so bad. When I'd finished, police had come
for Mr Woodhall, an ambulance had come for Mrs
Woodhall. Chinaski, when they slammed the front door
home, said, You still playing that Gypsy crap!

What do you know, he was right. I'd spent the night
writing out this tune, ``A Tzigan goes to town...'' I was all
played out and Chinaski refilled the glasses.

Percussion Drunk Piano

I should have been grateful. Many times in ma life, I should have been grateful, but since I feel resentful that I ever gotten lumbered with life anyways, I don't do gratitude that often. Chinaski didn't say much either as the firemen helped him down off the roof without asking too many questions. Didn't bat an eyelid, even when Chinaski asked to borrow an axe to break a skylight to steal some liquor. They just pulled the last Paki off ma head and advised me to see a casualty department. Chinaski said if I wasn't too groggy that I should ask the jerk jumping on ma head, ask him nice afore he got away, if his sister was seeing anybody. It didn't seem appropriate, last I saw of the youth was his wiry frame running back up the ginnel, baggy jumper and cheap flares billowing in the wind, probably his sister too was a bit on the skinny side and I like a chunk of woman to hold on cold nights. It was all Greek to Chinaski, uneyelid batted, trying to climb back up the ladder, with a chance-found stone, but the men in hats and a sideline in children's tv were having none of it. They'd got the call, arrived in under fifteen minutes and if they hadn't put a fire out, they hadn't done a bad job either. I had no complaints, Chinaski was down, the down and out was away and bumps on ma face was busting up, adding some sadistic interest to ma nondescript looks.

They didn't ring the bell as they drove off, leaving Chinaski and me in a bad part of town, by some shops without a tramp, but inside ma head a bell was ringing, shadows in ma corner with a cold sponge, urging me to get out there and finish what I hadn't started. I dug deep, pulled in a bruised lung of air and picked up ma gloves, ma feet and ... all ma arse. The only thing keeping me upright, in one body and mind and walking forwards was this fifty pence piece, anchored to ma fingers by something stronger than hope or love or ignorant desperation.

Chinaski was studying the graffiti on the side of the alley's wall. Two Asian matriarchs went by discussing *Coronation Street*: they sounded not unlike ma Grandma and her neighbour, Mrs Worn, though more eloquent, with a greater facility of the language of Shakespeare. It was time to get out of that part of town -- never liked it. Knew by the bumps on ma head, by that ancient occult science of phrenology, that if I was Paki and born here and living here I'd kick off too.

Chinaski thought we were going home. Said that he had a quart of whiskey stashed. I warned him that the stash was some *Bushmills* for ma father for Christmas and to leave it well alone. Chinaski bitched every step of the way back and I couldn't blame him. It looked like snow, the whole town went black and white with the light the clouds gave. It was time to hunch inside and walk fast. Despite cold, fancy footwork and the chiaroscuro effect, I wanted to brag to somebody about that discovery of Lowrie, that the northern industrial landscape was white not black. I wanted to act like I knew things, that I had had an education sometime, that I wasn't allus the way I am, stuttering bits of ma mind out into the open for all to look away at. MEMASTIGOMENOS, I shouted at a shadow of a car passing me at rush-hour pace. Chinaski pretended he was not with me. Under ma breath, holding the steam in, I mumbled over that word again, savouring its learned strangeness even though I never really kent what it meant.

I moved with ma breath of hidden word, tucked up gnosis, tongue-bitten and worn. I was making distance, making it back to the part of town where the panic attacks were fewer and your feet rustled with spent leaves of the chestnut trees above. I didn't care that Chinaski had punched a fat cyclist for ringing a bell at him. Chinaski bobbed and wove along the path and cycle-track and

114

someone fat was trying to cycle home, bell-ringing
insistent to get by, feeling a swift one in the ribs for his
trouble en passant, near passing out and away and along,
calling a breathless, mad cunt, in the air to make
Chinaski laugh and roar for more, leaves rustling behind
me towards the gloom, fat, lazy river knowing nothing,
hugging the path too as it swam by, leaving us to fumble
our way, through the maze of back streets, still with fifty
pence in ma fingers, itching to be spent on something
good.

I got thinking about fat. Chinaski had a thing with fat.
He'd punched two fat things I could remember. I couldn't
remember much. Perhaps it wasn't an issue, that rich
layer of body tissue, hugging the carcass of well fed bones.

We got there. Without killing anyone or even ourselves. We
got there to find that the butcher had sold out of bacon
bits for a pound. We got there to argue, Chinaski and I.

... Can't recall what I called Chinaski, but as ma
grandmother would say, It was very blue you know.
Chinaski took it for a while, took it till I said a word or
two too much, then he bent and buckled ma fingers back
till the fifty pence piece dropped. He picked it up, tried to
kick his head, but too slow and weak for that. Chinaski
flung that fat priest's fifty down the street into the dusk,
as I ran howling, howling ma heart out, groping in the
dark for just so damn long...howling even when I came
back where Chinaski stood in front of a fat butcher
begging for some bones to feed our dog, begging even as
the butcher locked up and told us to piss off, leaving us
totally in the dark, distant piss-yellow of streetlight by
yon corner: two men, one begging against a shut door; the
other, howling, howling real good as if he'd finally got the
hang of something at last, got it, got it good.

Dangling Tourniquet

There was a man in front of ma door. He was braying at it,
though not like a donkey. He tried a key, but I knew it
would do no good: I'd had the locks changed. It was ma
one good deed that year, something of which I was unduly
proud. The man banged on the door again. He ranted like
a Baptist preacher. It could only be ma landlord, but I
wouldn't feel sorry for him.

You after the tenant, I said. He replied that he was, looked
at me curiously. I said, smart, right off the cuff, I said this:
Don't tell me, I look just like him, that I look like ma
brother. I know that, everyone says that. Say, is he in?

The man who was ma landlord didn't reply. He shook and
kicked the door some more, then moved over to me in the
corridor. He just said one thing and I didn't think it was
all that witty, he said this: Either pay up, move out or I
send someone round with a baseball bat -- tell that to your
brother, you nut!

It was the last I saw of ma landlord. I don't think that we
said our goodbyes that properly. I don't think it was the
sort of goodbye that says we'll keep in touch, card at
Christmas, style. I didn't mind, fumbled with ma keys,
trying to open ma door to find that Chinaski had changed
the locks on me. Come back Bessie Smith.

Ham on Wry

It was cold, so cold, all them wet autumns we'd been having these last few years past made no odds, this fall was winter already, cold, cracked up cold, spilling silver over the ground, trees and rooftops and the twain of we, doing nothing but tasting hunger and burrowing down together in the crumpled swell of old sheets and blankets, trying to fight cold with metabolisms that couldn't keep a flea warm. We tasted hunger. We missed the rats.

Earlier in the week, Tuesday, perhaps earlier, I had found that a small pebble had worked its way into ma spent white trainers. I'd been annoyed at the time, seeing that the money that Chinaski had put behind the bookies' window wasn't coming back, that another horse had let me down, but that pebble, that pebble despite the mood I was in, had worked its way into ma pumps, worked its way agin my skin till I noticed, till I shook it out there and then inside the turf accountant's boarded up windows...There was something else I meant to say about that pebble but I've forgotten. To cut a long story short, I put it back. I let nature take its course. We walked away from the window, from the dead cert that Chinaski had in the next race and we walked all the way home, with this little pig having a pebble to keep it company.

Funny thing is, when we got in that pebble shook itself out and landed on the strip of carpet I still had left by ma bed. That pebble thought it had a home at last. So much for thinking, for as the second day of hunger struck I popped it in ma mouth for luck. It was there a good day and night afore Chinaski said, In the desert, you fool, in the desert you suck a pebble to help the thirst, that's what you suck a pebble for. I thought that Chinaski was just being crabby, as he wondered which finger-nail to bite next, 'cos no pebble had worked its way into his life, but

he took me down to the municipal library, skidding on ice,
watching old women break their calcium stripped hips,
took me down to the reference section to search through
this book on survival techniques.

Chinaski was right.

That night

I swallowed ma pebble,

felt thirsty, even as

fresh snow

fell.

Love, Bring me

I've lived a very meagre death, said Chinaski, bitching about the weather, the lack of food, and that was afore things got really bad. He said, Ring her up. I told Chinaski that I had no money. He believed me. He'd stolen the last of ma money for a horse that would not run fast enough for its jockey, its owner, and me. Go round then, said Chinaski. I told him to mind his own business. You gonna lose that girl, said Chinaski. You don't take her out. You go no where. You treat her to nothing. You not even that good in bed, whoever said you was must have been lying or desperate or just well paid -- you gotta get back in touch, said Chinaski.

Why, I said, you want to fuck her again?

Yeah, sure, said Chinaski.

How do you answer honesty like that? I turned over and looked at the wallpaper to see if I could see houses in it. At one time, I could look at any house in ma street and see a face or a personality in it. I could see goblins in wallpaper, strange owls in the folds of curtains and a woman that hanged herself by the shadow of the wardrobe. Ma mother did not take me to the psychiatrist then. I looked at the wallpaper, saw a damp patch that could have been a bride of Bernard Manning. I laughed at that. Chinaski didn't, he wondered who the hell was Bernard Manning, was he one that sold turkeys.

How do you answer ignorance like that? I turned over to look at the other wall, thought about ma favourite auntie who wondered why she had never heard of Stacy Kent.

Well, said Chinaski.

Well what, Stanley?

Quit, horsing around, you meet her from work.

Advice: I'd like to say that I walked through a shramming wind, through bitter rain and cold to see the girl I love walk out the cafe door to be met by a tall, dark handsome stranger, that they kissed lightly, that ma sweet girl didn't notice me huddled in the doorway opposite, watching on, love-torn voyeur, heart ripped in bits, but the old noble noggin saying, Ease up, heart, old buddy, she better off with him, then the torn heart agrees, stops hollering and after a while the rain stops, leaving me to walk back through puddles...I'd like to write you that scene, 'cos I want a head with sense and a tall, dark, handsome stranger to take care of ma sweet girl.

Can't answer masel' why the heartache I could write never hurt as much as the bland truth of: What the fuck you doing here? That's what ma sweet girl said, mouth like a sewer but still wanting kissing as I stood outside her posh cafe in the sleet with ma slippers on.

Something else I didn't have the answer for -- that last question of hers. I watched her walk away. I walked back through puddles, with heartburn and horripilation, some wiser, knowing that life ain't all unhappy fiction.

The Unloved Music
of Cold Water

There was the dull-slow sound of weeping falling through ma wall with the neighbours. Mr Goodhall was crying. I hoped it hurt. Chinaski wasn't in. He'd took off, said that he had to attend to a little business and when I pressed him over details he said, it was just like he said - his business.

Chinaski was an emphatic hijo de puta all right, all right.

Ma neighbour wept and I counted the seconds, watched them beat through ma walls in the shape of tears. After three minutes, five, I had enough, wondered again just what sort of business Chinaski could be cooking up.

It was none of ma concern, but you live with someone and pretty soon, their troubles end up bundled with your own. Still, none of ma concern.

Time-wrapped weeping drove me from ma room. I sat out on the front door step and watched a fraction of humanity wander in and out of vision. A whole bus-ful of lives stopped outside the door. They'd put a temporary stop in about two years back, ever since watched small, quiet unlovely lives unload in front of mi eyes, leaving me wondering if you could measure notions of permanence and temporality by a bus stop and its set of headscarfs, shopping, shoes and cheap sweat-shop clothes. Wondered how you'd carve up eternity by bus-queues; whether after a lifetime of mortality the afterlife and all that it promised came all at once queued up like so many 518s to Newcastle. I was wondering shit all sense whilst still thinking from time to time about the business interests of ma dead lodger. Who does he think he is to be having the like when dead...Chinaski once admitted to me that ever since he slipped off his slippers, he'd never been so well off, everyone wanted a piece of him now he was dead, reprints, new stuff, praise from critics that wouldn't have

121

wiped their dicks on him when alive, but now sang a chorus line of praise comic as a tragic Greek. Even when smug from answering one's own question, still I wondered, just what was he doing in this ghost town to have such a thing as a line of business.

It was none of ma concern.

I was concerned.

A cripple, the most beautiful cripple I'd ever seen stumbled off the bus. There was something ungainly, wooden and unyielding in her body: she didn't get off the bus, she made a leap for the pavement. She struck it hard and wandered off down-street, taking a lot of ma dirty thoughts with her. Like I say, she was beautiful. I took another measurement of time from ma father's watch. I clocked up the seconds deciding on a new ritual in ma life. I would wait for this bus, I would see if I could see this cripple girl again and her ungainly gait, smacking something determined against the face of pavements.

With a blue fart of diesel the bus pushed itself into the traffic, heading out of town. It was cold, small slithers of rain hitched down from clouds and the street was dull as only unloved northern streets can be. When I got back inside ma room, the crying had stopped, Chinaski had come in the back way, struggling over broken bits of bikes to threaten ma neighbour with something to cry about if he didn't quit hollering soon. Chinaski was back, I asked this, How's business? He smacked me in the nose, for an old man, for an old dead man, he could still pack a punch. I took out ma watch, counted down the seconds of water that ran from ma eyes. I could only manage thirty-nine seconds, thought about all that quality misery time that ma neighbour had been having of late, rubbed ma hands, blessed the second hand of a second-hand watch, satisfied with ma lot.

Say, if you really want to know, Chinaski started up...

122

In the Know
Business

Your problem is, said Chinaski, then took another dig at
the cheap bottle of wine that I'd stolen, your problem is
that you gave up 'fore you even born... Chinaski was in
ranting mood. Every time you get yourself something, you
give it away like you some kind of philanthropic
millionaire, as if love like that can be had like cheap
suites in a dollar store. You stick your stinky little cock in
and you go, "Hey, I look swell in this". Yeah, you get
yourself a new suit, and you happy for a while and then...

Chinaski preached it. He preached it all night:

remember the girl that loved you

even though you couldn't make her cum

remember the girl who gave all she had

you wouldn't take it away

remember the girl who'd forsake the Jews

for you

remember the girl who made you feel like

it was rape every time you touched her,

well she had love for you too

remember that tall Dane who lowered herself

to you

remember that rage of mad red hair who shat

out your bastard, still giving love to you

remember that heroin bitch who stole all you had,

fuck for a fix, fucked her head for you

remember the quiet girl who cried when she came

and screamed when you said you were through

remember the wrist-cutter

remember that lonely mother and her brain-damaged

daughter who sang to you.

Remember...

Chinaski was drunk with memories.

Chinaski sliced then fed me the past.

Chinaski talked the whole night through.

Nothing seemed to stay in ma mind, but ma step-father
finding me jigging school, 'cos I had the blues, said life
made no sense, life was a pile of shit, life was overrated.
Ma stepfather said, Well you gonna have a miserable
fucking life then. He weren't wrong. But mostly, this
fifteen seconds of now, I remembered that I once went to a
wedding in a dead man's suit.

All Time War

You gotta stop this, said Chinaski. It was five in the
morning. We were still drinking. I don't know how we
were affording this drinking, but it was all we had, so we
had it. We had our drinking in the lonely hours, those sad
hours savoured by the mad, the insomniacs and day-
haters. Those hours, black mould on the walls, no heating,
nothing in but drink, we had those hours cold as turkey,
shivering into our alcohol, getting chilled, mad laughing
one minute, biting chunks of spite the next -- we had those
hours; there was a hole in the window where we could
peak out at the moon. That gap had me thinking. I took
Chinaski out and sat him on the doorstep. I told him this:
-

Don't see her every day, but most evenings if I get the
chance, I get a smoke and I sit out here and watch a bus
arrive to leave people off and on that bus more times than
not, there is the world's most beautiful cripple and ma
hearts stops, don't know what to say to her, don't know
how to begin, how to say that I think she'd be a real cute,
beautiful fuck, that I'd want to do more than poke, more
than put a notch on ma belt to say I'd fucked a crip along
with the black, the half-caste, the Kraut, the Czech, the ...
it's not about that, hate all that -

For the love of God shut up, roared Chinaski. Why would
anyone want to fuck you, let alone a beautiful like that.
Who'd fuck a miserable, mad, sick, pissed up wreck like
you? Who do that without getting paid good money. You
make me sick. Chinaski undid his belt and there and
then, he whupped me on the front step in the quiet hours
so nobody would hear me whimper. Chinaski did that for
me, trying to shake some sense into me. I just waited till
his arm gotten tired, then I went for him.

I had him, had him where I wanted him, could have crippled him, could have done that, at least.

Carols
for a
Shithus

I am sitting on the front step, there's some hint of snow in the driving rain, but no quiet sleet yet. I should be smoking, but I'm giving it up, hate the way you have to mix baccy in with pot; hate the taste in the mouth it leaving, that and residual paranoia -- there's plenty to hate when all is said and done, especially yoursel'. Chinaski though is smoking. He don't mind ma hates this day or tomorrow's day. None of this is anything that concerns him.

There's that fart of steam...shat, compressed air, of the bus stopping. I look up to see ma beautiful cripple, the world's most beautiful cripple, hirple off the bus and harl her ungainly ass once more into life. There's brute lust and fear in ma mouth. She walking, she walking down the path to ma doorstep to where I sit with a dead man, smoking. She walks so that she can lay her shadow over me, shading out some shred of sun still left in the day. She looks down at me and spits. Stop looking, she says. Stop looking at me. She spits in ma face, cripple-spit in ma eyes. I look down from her face, beautiful still even in an ugly mood and I notice the mud on her boots. From ma back-pocket, take an old hanky, could be a wanky-hanky, could just be thick with old, cold snots; either way, I take the hanky, spit into it and clean and clean all traces of mud off her boots.

She slapped me. It felt good, even as stung blood flushed in ma face. It felt good, even as the she walked away, saying, You leave me alone now, you understand -- you leave me alone.

I watched her hirple her way away, liked what I saw.

Licked her spit off ma face, felt the coldness in the rain, with ma tongue, only with that did I sense how cold the day had really become.

Chinaski wanted to talk about this, sending a spit ball off into the wind and drawing again on his bitter smoke. And, if he didn't look warm, he did at least look content and he didn't have a young girl's spit on his face. Me, I had the cold company.

Just like the
Movies

There was a fat priest's fifty pence in ma hand and I knew
that with what I had already that there was clink enough
on me to buy masel' this bag of bacon bits from ma local
butcher. I was so happy. I walked with the quick, Chinaski
by ma side all along that path, smothered with leaves,
booby-trapped with dog shit, along the river to this road
that cut up to this street corner where the butcher man
was just shutting, he'd done for the day, he looked liked
he'd had enough, that maybe this shop wasn't paying too
well. Frankly, it appeared like the man had troubles, then
I asked him for a bag of bacon bits. Wiping his hands on
his stripy bib, he said that he had sold out of bacon bits,
but that maybe he'd have some more in, come the end of
the week, and was there anything else that I would like
instead...He could have said something else, but I tore into
Chinaski, like cheating lovers, we had it out there and
then, the argument spilling outside, till Chinaski knocked
me to the ground, jumped on my hand, till ma fingers
uncurled, till they let loose of that fat priest's fifty pence.
Chinaski took the coin and he threw it out into the
darkness of the street, ill-lit by lamplight, all soft yellow
weeping night.

Picking masel' off the pavement, I went back in, I said to
the man just closing his shop if he would have such a
thing as a bag of bones to give to ma dog. Chinaski
reminded me that in terms of the rent agreement I was
not allowed to keep pets.

We left it like that

a perplexed butcher

wiping his hands

on an apron,

a small sum of money

lost in the dark,

me without a dog

to bring along

home.

Old Time Stewed:
Songs
Stories
Poems
&
More Truthful
Confabulations

You know, we are sitting there, on the doorstep, waiting
for snow to fall. Can sense it, when it's in the air, sinuses
sort of leak out the news to ma brain that snow is coming.
It's cold enough for snow, anyways. It's cold enough for
hell, truth told. That Scandinavian Hell, that Dante's Hell,
with frozen hearts, that Hell, that sees a pensioner slip
and fall outside ma gate spilling the messages,
septuagenarian oaths and stained dentures. We laughed,
even as we slipped and fell, helping that lady up, we
laughed, for the raw madness of it.

'Spose you think this is funny, well, wait till you get to ma
age, ma lad, then we'll see `ow much you damn well laugh
then -- this is what the old lady said.

Well that's as maybe, ma'am, but you sure as hell won't be
there to see us laughing -- that is what Chinaski said.

I had stopped laughing, by then, thought that it could
have been ma own gran we laughing at, and anyways in
the first laugh, I just laughed through nerves and raw
madness, nothing worse, nothing more. As for Chinaski, I
could never be sure what truly made him laugh...or even,
for what it is worth, what made him cry.

I know for certain that he helped the old lady home,
bitching all the way, but helping her more than anyone
else in that road, including me. Something had gone. All I

want to do, is sit on this step and see time pass, see the
seconds go by, perhaps peppered with a little snow. It sure
smelt like snow out there on that step, nursing a mug
with a tea bag in it, stewed and stewed again, but at least
off the drink, so far that morning. I don't even like tea
bags. I like real tea. I like a real woman as opposed to
wanking memories, but sometimes that is just the way it
is.

He was back. Could be. Couldn't be sure. But, a man with
a baseball bat was back looking for someone that, at least
going by the photograph, was me. He said, See that. I saw.
This you? he said. Nay, that's ma brother, I said. You sure?
he said. Are you? I said.

For a while he left it like that, I think he was hoping that
I would crack: the way he bounced the baseball bat in his
hands, and stared hard down at me, huddled around ma
tea bag. It worked. After a while, I said, Look do you think
I would sit on this step, outside in the cold, if I could be on
the inside of that room of ma brother's all snug and
warm? Do you think, I'd sit here when there's snow
coming along any second soon, do you think I would be so
stupid to do that?

He took me by surprise. Nay. He didn't strike out. He
didn't hurt me. He just said that his boyfriend was like
that, that he too could smell snow. He'd go all sniffly, bit
stuffy in the head and say that they'd be snow along soon,
most times he was right. He also said that I was not to get
ideas, that just 'cos he was gay that it didn't mean he
wouldn't smack ma head with a baseball bat. This was
business.

There was still no sign of the snow, I was sick of the
company. I reached inside the door and pulled out a stack
of letters, many of them urgent, many of them important
letters that ought to be read, I said, Look, charva, if I was
in, don't you think that rather than sit on this cold step,

waiting for snow, that I would at least read some of these letters, some of the important ones, all marked in red?

That I think impressed him of ma basic underlying honesty. He sloped off, promising to be back, that I was to warn ma brother to pay his bills, and that if he ever had to come back, and I was here and ma brother not, then he'd bat me just the same, 'cos it was getting to that stage, that someone soon just had to be batted. He walked away while I began to read some of ma mail. I'd missed two important appointments at the hospital, pretty soon they'd come looking, too. There were other reminders and a hostile letter from someone who claimed to know something about me, about some of the lies they spread and like to believe about me; all this written and no one even asked ma paranoia to sit down and give them a hand -- beautiful coincidence.

He was back. Chinaski that is. He came back. He said, What do you know, that old bitch didn't even offer me a cup of tea, after I half carried her back. I passed over ma mug. He passed me a bottle of sweet sherry that he'd stolen from somewhere. We sat outside for a good while, waiting for the snow to show up soon.

Last Poem Earth

There it was.

Chinaski up on ma bed.

There I was.

None the wiser.

Till

Chinaski said,

It's the guts that go first.

Wiser than a salmon.

Ma head still stuck

necking a bottle

till

Chinaski said,

Not your head,

nervous system,

marriage

or

mortgage,

but nothing

like that,

134

just the guts,

they go first.

I hiccupped

a bit of sick.

I spit a bit

of spit.

There it was.

I drank some more.

Chinaski threw

on to ma lap

his old pair

of boxer shorts

still warm

with

shit.

There it was.

Advice

at last. And I drank.

Hunted
with
the
Runted

You know they say

Mrs Goodhall has gone.

Still don't know if I got her name

right.

Thinking about this, 'cos it is three-thirty in the morning,
and it's cold, it's so cold, couldn't doss on ma step today,
not even with a dead poet, too much snow, piled up cold
outside. Some suit, some suit, with a future, a wife, no
doubt a pension plan, well, he says on ma small portable
wireless that there is a cold snap coming in. You see what
happened is that there was this warm low moving in off
the Atlantic, it picked up a lot of warm humid disposition
off the Azores, then drifted our way. What that warm
schmuck of air didn't know was that soon as it harled its
ass over ma here, then some sudden change of wind would
bring cold Siberian chill straight off the north east coast to
churn that wet moist stuff into cold floating Hell.

Snow it arrived

at ma door

piled up

plentiful as poverty

free for all

a bargain store

Christ

but not allus with us.

There's cold outside. It waits. It endures its own depth. It has me freezing, huddled in all ma clothes. Out of a cracked window, I see that all looks like it's queued up for one of those magical little moments from Joyce. That looking on that blanket of cooled rain I should all of a sudden get ma life and death together -- see it all in a moment, pristine, clear and about 6 below.

What I see is Chinaski on the bed, biting his toenails, 'cos he's supple that way and we don't have nail scissors. As for masel,' I fancy some kind of fancy irony. I want to get out ma old busted clarinet and play "Jingle Bells" to a cracked window in memory of the late great James Joyce. Who is truly dead, dead as snow.

It was this small desire that had me thinking of Mrs Goodhall. What she doing now? Who with? Why? Does she enjoy it? Does it beat getting smacked around by her old man? I miss her. Don't miss hearing her hurting.

It's early morning, no one too near to wake with ma dirge. I look under the bed to fall upon only ma Chinese broadsword. Can't find ma clarinet. Can't find ma soprano sax. I go mad for a while looking. Then I ask Chinaski, who is trying to pop a bad blister with the red-eye of a joint, if he has seen ma musical instruments.

Chinaski says, Son, who do you think has been feeding you with beer. Where did you think I got the money for for the drink, the smoke, that mobile phone and a couple of hot tips over the sticks?

I cried.

Chinaski had sold ma instruments for

fuck all.

He could never know

what he had done,

not even by looking at

snow.

I cried when he told me

the news

about all those 'osses

failing fast,

letting me

down.

I cried,

It's allus the damn 'osses

damn dog-meat on legs

damn 'osses!

Be a man,

Chinaski said,

Leave those fine beasts alone.

I wiped ma tears on ma orange curtains. I looked out at
the snow, lying thick and solid as ma dreams, and I
whistled "Jingle Bells" as I envied the quick and the dead,
as Chinaski, cleaned the wax out of his ears with the
corner of ma eiderdown.

Pulp-it

They tried to see me today.
Two social workers
and a doctor. They tried
to do me some good,
even as I explained
that I wasn't there,
that I had moved on,
that perhaps it was
ma brother they were
looking for. They tried
to get through ma door.
Even as I spun ma best
lies. Oh they tried,
even as I sent in Chinaski
who told them all
where they could go.
They tried at least
for a while, but, see,
you can't argue
with a dead man,
no matter how hard
you try. But
They tried.

Shakespeare
Doing the Double

Through the snow two foot deep, a man came calling
today. He tried to impress upon me that he was ma
brother, that he had been worried about me, that perhaps
I should try to come home. I said, if you are really ma
brother, then you had better take ma mail, and watch out
around here, 'cos the landlord wants a word, and some
hard gay nut wants to put pieces of your brain on his
baseball bat. I said, brother to brother, that if you were
really ma Cain, then I am unable to help. He left without
another word, though at door, by the drifting snow,
Chinaski touched him for a fiver.

I worry.

They are on to me.

All of them.

Even Chinaski.

Even ma brother.

Even me.

Luck Makes
a Poor
Living

I write tunes no one will play. I make music not for masel,'
but I've never met ma listener. Spent years studying
composition, for ma work to be chewed by mice, rotting in
plastic bags, growing mould, becoming damp, obsolete
afore a performance call; much of it half-made, half of it
will never be finished. Spent ma life, playing music. Spent
time, listening to all that I could. Taught composition to a
child for some school exam. This bairn grown up and doing
well. Yesterday on the wireless, there was a piece written
by this person. It wasn't bad, it wasn't astounding, but it
was performed, broadcast and the start of something more
promising. I write and play music -- it is a sakeless task.

Today, I play a penny whistle. My instruments have all
been sold. I play a penny whistle in the key of D. I would
sooner have the penny than this whistle.

Chinaski shuffles around ma room like a bear, shambolic
with the dregs of hibernation. He is not well. It is cold as
old bones in here. There's ice on the inside of the window.
This is something, 'cos there ain't much window left. It's
cold in here. I play on ma penny whistle, Chinaski shuffles
like a bear, if more people came by, I would put ma hat
down, try to collect some heaven-sent pennies.

It's so cold, I could beg.

Musing on Betting

Take me back to that cheap washeretta where the poor people go, take me back there, please, said Chinaski. He was shivering up, burning bad, seemed like he had malaria, but just body busted with cold. It was as if he was dying all over again. We had lain in bed for two days solid, barely getting up, save to piss -- too cold to shit. We just farted bad under the covers and cursed each other. It was cold, small pool of snow fallen from the hole in the window. Good shot, God, good shot, ma man.

Take me back to that tumble dryer. Let's go there. Let's step inside and warm up some. Let's go to a petrol station, squirt juice all over each other and drop the match. Let's go, let's go, said Chinaski. But it was too cold to move anywhere. I wasn't shifting, besides with Chinaski burning up, it got almost warm in there.

Chinaski, said something, said something quiet, so much low, in fact, that I thought he was just delirium mumbling. Chinaski said, Who's your favourite poet? I said I hate 'em all. Chinaski laughed then, laughed good and proper. I knew he'd pull through then, anyone with fire in the belly still to dislikes poets wasn't dead yet.

Then Chinaski said, Where did your sweet girl go?

There was cold in ma stomach. Burning cold khusty for dossin'.

Bone Dancing

Late, early morning, oxymoron, contradiction in terms,
cold, quiet, door creaking, light on and ma sweet woman
there, pissed, painted up nice, ma keys in her hand.
Bastard, said ma sweet girl. I couldn't count the days
since I saw her last. But, she didn't talk that hate, even
when drunk. Bastard, she said again, then the real words
came. Chinaski, shivering still, took himself to the toilet,
wrapped in a blanket, looking like something from the
IRA's dirty campaign, leaving me with her words.

Why didn't you come and see me? Why? All right, I was
out of order, but why? You said you loved me. You dumped
me. You went back with that lass who had your abortion.
And you didn't want her to. You still love that Jewish
bitch, she had an abortion. You went back out with that
lass that cheated on you with that nigger. You stuck with
that heroin addict who stole your money and sucked
people off for money or a fix. You went out with someone
even though you knew she was seeing her old boyfriend.
You...

It went on for a while longer. Ma past, ma whole
illustrious career as a mug, aborted out in pieces of hate,
from a girl, drunk and hurt and still looking lovely. She
sat on ma bed, cried and tried not to cry. She moved on to
something else.

Went out with Trace and Shona. Went clubbing. I got
pissed. I tapped off. We did it...did it in the bogs. It was
crap...it was fucking horrible.

A man, a better man than me at this point, would have
put an arm around her. Ma step-father, a small bull of a
man, would have done something right. Ma grandad was
dead and in the grave and nothing but small tears

pearling from ma eyes and ma step-father came up to me, put an arm, thick as a bough about ma shoulders, said, Come on along, son. Someone special would have found some words to salve or shrive this situation. But, I waited, watching her cry, licking ma pain; watched her walk away.

When Chinaski came back in. I asked him to turn off the light afore getting bedded down again. He grumbled, but that's all.

Out to Lunch
at the Captain's Table

The cold is slow. It's grip when you live with it all the time, is not sudden, not an ache, but a long dull pain. It has you none the less. Worried sick about Chinaski. His skin all pale purple, flaking and paper-thin. It's bad in this room. Can't let it get worse. The cold is slow, but it catches up; it gets there in the end, only, slowly.

There's a small grate. It's been boarded up a long time. Occasionally, I'd hear small smutts fall, a jackdaw once got trapped behind, took me a while to pull off the panel and let the bird out. It squawked soot over ma room, flew around demented, till I threw an old dictionary at it. Felt bad about that, bad and very stupid.

The panel comes away easily. I get out ma sheet music. I ball it up. I make a small pyre, then break up the board and put it on top. It looks right, it looks sea-worthy and Bristol fashion. So I light it. The first match fails, as does the second, on the third there is a little more joy. A glow curls into a flame. The flame spreads. There is a bit of heat, a bit of fire. That's when I really go to town. Anything I can find in there. Ma old music. It's on. It's singing flames.

Chinaski stirs, gives me a hand. We're sweating. We're warm. We drink the last of our drink as we cram that fireplace tight.

We dance. Get that. By a warm hearth we dance, shout, sing and drink. Small good thing.

Don't bother with the covers. We flop on the bed. Sleep.

Confusion is raw shouts of voices and air quickened with

smoke. Surprise is the silhouettes framed in the doorway. Panic is some idiot scrambling under the bed searching for a Chinese broadsword. Insanity is the man waving the sword above his head, shouting you'll never take me alive: shouting, I work for the triads, I am a master of Chut Sing Tong Long. Remorse is sitting outside in a blanket watching a house burn with neighbours and engines all around. Happenstance is being recognised by a bystander with a baseball bat. Concussion is...

Sun Burns
out of Reach

The psychiatrist says that he wants to help. He wants to know why I set fire to that place. He wants to find out why I would wish to kill masel'.

He prescribes Haldol.

I take three in the mornings.

I take three in the afternoons.

I take three at night with a cup of weak drinking chocolate.

It's all dulled up and slow and I've lost Chinaski.

The psychiatrist has more questions along with the old. I can't seem to find anyone to answer his presumptions for him.

He prescribes plugging me into the mains.

Wake with a bang. It's ma head. A lovely nurse is helping me in recovering. Christ ma throat is dry. She holds ma hand. I wish she'd hold ma dick. I wish someone would. Feel so lonely.

They put me in a new ward with a day room. There I find him. Old Chinaski is there, by the window, a book, flapping in his hands, unread, his eyes smiling out at the lawns.

Chinaski, you fucker, I say. He's mad, bitching and sulking saying. I say, Aw snap out of it, Chinaski, it's me. Promise I'll never leave you again. I'm sorry about that.

I draw up a chair. Me and Chinaski are back. He not saying anything. It's a change I'm concerned about, so I go and tell him all the crazy things we've been up to and he still gives nothing back. Just a book flapping in his arms like a lame dove. I do this all afternoon till a male nurse says, Is he bothering you?

I tell him to get fucked. They drag me off to give me a jab. Last thing I shout, is don't worry, Chinaski, I'm coming back.

What Matters Most

I didn't walk through the fire. I was carried. On the back of a fireman, ranting, waving a broadsword, swearing to fight them all, that is how I left ma burning home. I tell the psychiatrist this. She doesn't say much. She never says anything. Two notes. I saw her write two notes, afore she said I could go back to the day room to where I find Chinaski still seated by the window, looking out on the lawns like they emptied his eyes, that book still flitting in his hands. It could be the same day, it could be yesterday or next year. Won't leave him, though.

Chinaski, it's me, said I would be back. This is what I say, pulling up a chair, prepared to be patient. At first I don't realise that Chinaski is speaking, just mumbling, just lips twitching, but there's definite words there. He says, Son, you've got to get out. No way, Chinaski, you mudfuck fraud, you're coming with me, I said. Chinaski's hand, all tremble and shakes moves over slow and grabs ma hand. He says, Look around -- you gotta go. I look. Seeing that room, I see it all. The whole room is full of Chinaskis and none of them are gonna get out. Then I cry. Then I try all the windows and doors. Locked.

I sit by Chinaski. I sit for a while, then throw his book out of the window, never could stand Jane Austen.

It's visitors. I hear a voice that I almost recognise. I turn and Mrs Woodhall is at the door, getting let in, asking to see me. I run over, grab a hand. She says, NO, not you, you're not ma friend. Ma friend is over there. She points at Chinaski. She brushes past. She brushes her body against mine, feel her breast, feel her large warm thigh, she pulls me towards her. Run, you fool, she whispers, then continues to make her way to the man without a book in his hands.

There's a door about to close, but I'm through it, through it and running. I smack the corridors with ma feet. I run a rats maze of behaviourism, finding the kitchens, an unlocked fire-exit and the place where they store the bins. I run, run, run as fast as I can, you can't catch me I'm the Gingerman. I run it. All the way out and onto the busy road leading into town. Side-stepping tourists, shoppers and the ubiquitous dog shit -- elegant, elegant as a rugby league layker -- I make it to the dead hub of touristville, this dead Disneyfied town. I run, find ma girl, ma sweet woman in her uniform working a table. Stop to peer in, through that big goldfish bowl of conspicuous consolation, see 'em munching on ersatz Edwaaaaardianism -- dick n jin, charvo. See ma sweet girl turn. She sees me. She sorts of smiles. She looks me up and down, shakes her head and gives me the finger. Can't help but laugh. On her finger are the keys to ma burnt down home. She laughs back. This is good. So happy that I burnt that shit-hole down, but I mun still run.

Feet they ache, feet they sore -- what else can you expect when you're made out of gingerbread. I miss Chinaski, Mrs Goodhall, ma sweet woman -- guess I'm gonna miss 'em all bad-bad...but I'm still running of that I am sure. It rains. I'm running, free-running as salt, through the streets, across this town, even as I turn to mush, legs wobble and break, I ain't gonna stop till I run off the page.